Washington Square

華盛頓廣場

商務印書館

Name of Book: Washington Square
Author: Henry James
Retold: Gina D. B. Clemen
Activities: Anna Maria Patrone
Editor: Rebecca Raynes
Design: Nadia Maestri
Illustrations: Ivan Canu
Edition: ©1999 Black Cat Publishing
          an imprint of Cideb Editrice, Genoa, Canterbury

系 列 名：Black Cat 優質英語階梯閱讀 · Level 5
書　　名：華盛頓廣場
顧　　問：Angeli Lau
責任編輯：傅　伊
封面設計：張　毅　曹　磊
出　　版：商務印書館（香港）有限公司
　　　　　香港筲箕灣耀興道3號東滙廣場8樓
　　　　　http://www.commercialpress.com.hk
印　　刷：中華商務彩色印刷有限公司
　　　　　香港新界大埔汀麗路36號中華商務印刷大廈
版　　次：2003年8月第1版第1次印刷
　　　　　© 2003 商務印書館（香港）有限公司
　　　　　ISBN 962 07 1667 1
　　　　　Printed in Hong Kong

出版説明

　　本館一向倡導優質閱讀，近年來連續推出了以 "Q" 為標識的 "Quality English Learning 優質英語學習" 系列，其中《讀名著學英語》叢書，更是香港書展入選好書，讀者反響令人鼓舞。推動社會閱讀風氣，推動英語經典閱讀，藉閱讀拓廣世界視野，提高英語水平，已經成為一種潮流。

　　然良好閱讀習慣的養成非一日之功，大多數初、中級程度的讀者，常視直接閱讀厚重的原著為畏途。如何給年輕的讀者提供切實的指引和幫助，如何既提供優質的學習素材，又提供名師的教學方法，是當下社會關注的重要問題。針對這種情況，本館特別延請香港名校名師，根據多年豐富的教學經驗，精選海外適合初、中級英語程度讀者的優質經典讀物，有系統地出版了這套叢書，名為《Black Cat 優質英語階梯閱讀》。

　　《Black Cat 優質英語階梯閱讀》體現了香港名校名師堅持經典學習的教學理念，以及多年行之有效的學習方法。既有經過改寫和縮寫的經典名著，又有富創意的現代作品；既有精心設計的聽、說、讀、寫綜合練習，又有豐富的歷史文化知識；既有彩色插圖、繪圖和照片，又有英美專業演員朗讀作品的 CD。適合口味不同的讀者享受閱讀之樂，欣賞經典之美。

　　《Black Cat 優質英語階梯閱讀》由淺入深，逐階提升，好像參與一個尋寶遊戲，入門並不難，但要真正尋得寶藏，需要投入，更需要堅持。只有置身其中的人，才能體味純正英語的魅力，領略得到真實的快樂。當英語閱讀成為自己生活的一部分，英語水平的提高自然水到渠成。

商務印書館 (香港) 有限公司
編輯部

使用説明

⬥ 應該怎樣選書？

按閱讀興趣選書

《Black Cat 優質英語階梯閱讀》精選世界經典作品，也包括富於創意的現代作品；既有膾炙人口的小説、戲劇，又有非小説類的文化知識讀物，品種豐富，內容多樣，適合口味不同的讀者挑選自己感興趣的書，享受閱讀的樂趣。

按英語程度選書

《Black Cat 優質英語階梯閱讀》現設 Level 1 至 Level 6，由淺入深，涵蓋初、中級英語程度。讀物分級採用了國際上通用的劃分標準，主要以詞彙（vocabulary）和結構（structures）劃分。

Level 1 至 Level 3 出現的詞彙較淺顯，相對深的核心詞彙均配上中文解釋，節省讀者查找詞典的時間，以專心理解正文內容。在註釋的幫助下，讀者若能流暢地閱讀正文內容，就不用擔心這一本書程度過深。

Level 1 至 Level 3 出現的動詞時態形式和句子結構比較簡單。動詞時態形式以現在時（present simple）、現在時進行式（present continuous）、過去時（past simple）為主，句子結構大部分是簡單句（simple sentences）。此外，還包括比較級和最高級（comparative and superlative forms）、可數和不可數名詞（countable and uncountable nouns）以及冠詞（articles）等語法知識點。

Level 4 至 Level 6 出現的動詞時態形式，以現在完成時（present perfect）、現在完成時進行式（present perfect continuous）、過去完成時（past perfect continuous）為主，句子結構大部分是複合句（compound sentences）、條件從句（1st and 2nd conditional sentences）等。此外，還包括情態動詞（modal verbs）、被動形式（passive forms）、動名詞（gerunds）、

短語動詞（phrasal verbs）等語法知識點。

　　根據上述的語法範圍，讀者可按自己實際的英語水平，如詞彙量、語法知識、理解能力、閱讀能力等自主選擇，不再受制於學校年級劃分或學歷高低的約束，完全根據個人需要選擇合適的讀物。

❷ 怎樣提高閱讀效果？

　　閱讀的方法主要有兩種：一是泛讀，二是精讀。兩者各有功能，適當地結合使用，相輔相成，有事半功倍之效。

　　泛讀，指閱讀大量適合自己程度（可稍淺，但不能過深）、不同內容、風格、體裁的讀物，但求明白內容大意，不用花費太多時間鑽研細節，主要作用是多接觸英語，減輕對它的生疏感，鞏固以前所學過的英語，讓腦子在潛意識中吸收詞彙用法、語法結構等。

　　精讀，指小心認真地閱讀內容精彩、組織有條理、遣詞造句又正確的作品，着重點在於理解 "準確" 及 "深入"，欣賞其精彩獨到之處。精讀時，可充分利用書中精心設計的練習，學習掌握有用的英語詞彙和語法知識。精讀後，可再花十分鐘朗讀其中一小段有趣的文字，邊唸邊細心領會文字的結構和意思。

　　《Black Cat 優質英語階梯閱讀》中的作品均值得精讀，如時間有限，不妨嘗試每兩個星期泛讀一本，輔以每星期挑選書中一章精彩的文字精讀。要學好英語，持之以恆地泛讀和精讀英文是最有效的方法。

❸ 本系列的練習與測試有何功能？

　　《Black Cat 優質英語階梯閱讀》特別注重練習的設計，為讀者考慮周到，切合實用需求，學習功能強。每章後均配有訓練聽、說、讀、寫四項技能的練習，分量、難度恰到好處。

聽力練習分兩類，一是重聽故事回答問題，二是聆聽主角對話、書信朗讀、或模擬記者訪問後寫出答案，旨在以生活化的練習形式逐步提高聽力。每本書均配有 CD 提供作品朗讀，朗讀者都是專業演員，英國作品由英國演員錄音，美國作品由美國演員錄音，務求增加聆聽的真實感和感染力。多聆聽英式和美式英語兩種發音，可讓讀者熟悉二者的差異，逐漸培養分辨英美發音的能力，提高聆聽理解的準確度。此外，模仿錄音朗讀故事或模仿主人翁在戲劇中的對白，都是訓練口語能力的好方法。

閱讀理解練習形式多樣化，有縱橫字謎、配對、填空、字句重組等等，注重訓練讀者的理解、推敲和聯想等多種閱讀技能。

寫作練習尤具新意，教讀者使用網式圖示（spidergrams）記錄重點，採用問答、書信、電報、記者採訪等多樣化形式，鼓勵讀者動手寫作。

書後更設有升級測試（Exit Test）及答案，供讀者檢查學習效果。充分利用書中的練習和測試，可全面提升聽、說、讀、寫四項技能。

④ 本系列還能提供甚麼幫助？

《Black Cat 優質英語階梯閱讀》提倡豐富多元的現代閱讀，巧用書中提供的資訊，有助於提升英語理解力，擴闊視野。

每本書都設有專章介紹相關的歷史文化知識，經典名著更有作者生平、社會背景等資訊。書內富有表現力的彩色插圖、繪圖和照片，使閱讀充滿趣味，部分加上如何解讀古典名畫的指導，增長見識。有的書還提供一些與主題相關的網址，比如關於不同國家的節慶源流的網址，讓讀者多利用網上資源增進知識。

Contents

Part of the story is recorded. 故事選錄

 These symbols indicate the beginning and end of the extracts linked
to the listening activities. 聽力練習開始和結束的標記

A Note on Henry James

Henry James was born on 15 April 1843, at 21 Washington Place, New York, of Irish and Scottish ancestry. [1] He was the second of five children, four boys and one girl.

His father, Henry James senior, was a prominent theologian [2] and philosopher. He had strong views on how children should be educated, and Henry James and his brothers and sister spent their formative [3] years in Europe. His brother William became an important psychologist and philosopher.

In 1862 Henry James entered Harvard Law School. Encouraged by his friend, William Dean Howells, who was to become another famous American writer, he began to write short stories and reviews for American journals.

---

1. **ancestry** : all of a person's ancestors.
2. **theologian** : expert in study of religion.
3. **formative** : having an important and lasting influence on a person's character.

A Note on Henry James

James found America to be hostile towards creative talent, and in 1869 he left the United States and spent a year travelling in England, France and Italy.

In 1875 after two prior visits to Europe he settled for a year in Paris. In Paris he met Flaubert, Turgenev and other important writers of that time. James's supreme master was Balzac, whom he greatly admired. The next year he moved to London, where he became very popular. London was his home for the next twenty years. During the next decade James wrote some of his best works, *Daisy Miller* (1879), *Washington Square* (1881), *The Portrait of a Lady* (1882) and *The Bostonians* (1886).

He wrote twenty novels and nearly one hundred short stories. James also tried writing plays, but he was not very successful.

His later works include *What Maisie Knew* (1897), *The Awkward Age* (1899), *The Wings of the Dove* (1902), *The Ambassadors* (1903) and *The Golden Bowl* (1904).

In 1915 James became a naturalized [1] British citizen. On New Year's Day 1916 he received the certificate of the Order of Merit, [2] and died on 28 February of the same year.

Henry James remains one of the greatest and most influential literary figures of the realist tradition. His realism can be called "psychological realism" because it deals with the human mind, the soul and existence. *Washington Square* is a superb [3] example of 19th century American realism.

---

1. **naturalized** : allowed to become a citizen of a country where somebody was not born.
2. **Order of Merit** : an order founded in 1902 for distinguished achievement.
3. **superb** : excellent.

James's house.

Henry James and his brother William James, by Marie Leon.

1 **After you have read Henry James's short biography, read the following sentences and put them in the correct order.**

a. His father sent him and his brothers and sister to Europe where they spent their formative years.

b. While he was at Harvard, a friend encouraged him to write short stories and reviews for American journals.

c. The following year he received the Order of Merit but died shortly afterwards.

d. In 1875 he spent a year in Paris where he met many important writers of the time.

e. Henry James was born in 1843 in New York.

f. Henry James entered Harvard Law School in 1862.

g. He left Paris for London where he lived for twenty years.

h. In 1915 he became a naturalized British citizen.

CHAPTER 1

Doctor Sloper

uring the first half of the nineteenth century a very distinguished physician [1] lived in the city of New York. Doctor Austin Sloper had acquired an impeccable [2] reputation as a doctor, because he was not only intelligent, honest and skilled, [3] but he also knew how to please his patients. Every patient received a long, detailed explanation about the ailment, [4] accompanied by an illegible [5] prescription. [6] His patients considered him the cleverest doctor in the country.

At the time that we are concerned with him, Doctor Sloper

---

1. **physician** : formal word for doctor.
2. **impeccable** : perfect.
3. **skilled** : having great ability in his work.
4. **ailment** : illness.
5. **illegible** : difficult or impossible to read.
6. **prescription** : written order for medicine.

was fifty years old and was an influential part of the best society of New York City. His wit, [1] intelligence and brilliant conversation made him the centre of attention at all fashionable parties.

In 1820 he had had the good fortune of falling in love with and marrying Catherine Harrington, a very charming and beautiful heiress. [2] She had a fortune [3] of $10,000 a year, but Austin Sloper was completely indifferent [4] to this fact. His goal

1. **wit** : ability to say things that are clever and amusing.
2. **heiress** : a woman who will inherit a lot of property or money.
3. **fortune** : wealth, great amount of money or property.
4. **indifferent** : not interested in something.

in life was to become a successful physician and to acquire a lot of professional experience. He was very fond of his profession and worked diligently to achieve [1] his goal.

Part of his professional experience, however, was quite unwelcome. [2] His first child, a little boy of extraordinary promise, died at the age of three. Neither the mother's love nor the father's science saved him.

Two years later Mrs Sloper had a second child, a little girl. The fact that the child was a girl, and not a boy, greatly disappointed the Doctor. It had been his dream to make an admirable man out of the little boy. But then something worse happened. A week after the child's birth the young wife fell ill and died, leaving Doctor Sloper alone with the little girl, whom he named Catherine after her mother.

For a man whose profession was to keep people alive, Doctor Sloper had failed with his own family. However, no one criticised him but himself. He blamed [3] himself and bore [4] the weight of this blame all his life.

Catherine grew up to be a robust, [5] healthy child and Doctor Sloper had no fear of losing *her*. When Catherine was about ten years old, Doctor Sloper invited his sister, Mrs Lavinia Penniman, to stay with him.

---

1. **achieve** : obtain.
2. **unwelcome** : unpleasant.
3. **blamed** : considered someone responsible for something bad.
4. **bore** : *(bear, bore, borne)* carried.
5. **robust** : healthy and strong.

He had two sisters who had both married early in life. The younger one, Mrs Elizabeth Almond, was the wife of a prosperous merchant and the mother of a large family. Mrs Almond was an attractive, reasonable [1] woman.

The Doctor preferred her to his other sister Lavinia, who had married a poor and sickly [2] clergyman. [3] The clergyman had died at the age of thirty-three, leaving Lavinia without children and without fortune.

Doctor Sloper had not invited his sister to live with him forever. He had suggested that she look for lodgings [4] while she stayed with him. It is uncertain whether Mrs Penniman ever looked for lodgings, but it is certain that she never found them.

Mrs Penniman settled with her brother and never went away. After six months Doctor Sloper accepted the fact. She explained to everyone, except Doctor Sloper, that she was in charge of Catherine's education. His opinion of women in general was not high, and he felt his sister did not possess any intellectual gifts. In his life the Doctor had admired only one woman—his wife.

He was always extremely polite to Lavinia, but he never discussed anything of importance with her. Once when Catherine was about twelve years old he had said to her, "Try and make a clever woman out of her, Lavinia. I should like her to be a clever woman."

---

1. **reasonable** : sensible.
2. **sickly** : not healthy.
3. **clergyman** : Protestant priest.
4. **lodgings** : room(s) that one pays rent for in a private house.

Doctor Hoper

Mrs Penniman looked at him thoughtfully and said, "My dear Austin, do you think it is better to be clever than to be good?"

"Good for what?" asked the Doctor. "You are good for nothing unless you are clever. Of course, I wish Catherine to be good, but she will not be a better person if she is a fool."

Mrs Penniman was a tall, thin, fair woman with a pleasant disposition. [1] She was romantic and sentimental, with a passion for little secrets and mysteries. She had never had a lover, but dreamed of having one and writing to him.

Her brother, who was very astute, [2] could read her thoughts and said to himself, "When Catherine is about seventeen years old, Lavinia will try and persuade her that some young man with a moustache [3] is in love with her. It will be quite untrue. No young man, with or without a moustache, will ever be in love with Catherine. Fortunately, Catherine isn't a romantic person."

Catherine was healthy, well built and large. She completely lacked her mother's beauty, her father's intelligence and was definitely not clever. She was not ugly, she simply had a plain, [4] dull aspect with her brown hair, thick features and small, quiet eyes.

---

1. **disposition** : the way that a person tends to behave or feel.
2. **astute** : clever and quick at seeing how to gain an advantage.

3. **moustache** :

4. **plain** : ordinary.

Washington Square

Catherine was extremely fond of her father and very much afraid of him. She was a good, docile, [1] obedient and affectionate [2] daughter, whose deepest desire and greatest happiness was to please her father.

Although Catherine never knew it, she was a total disappointment for Doctor Sloper, who would have liked a daughter to be proud of. There was nothing to be ashamed of [3] in poor Catherine, but this was not enough for the Doctor, who was a proud man.

She was neither pretty, elegant, nor charming, and by the age of eighteen Mrs Penniman had not succeeded in making her a clever woman.

At social events she was very quiet and insignificant. She was never the centre of attention. The kinder friends of Doctor Sloper described Catherine as lady-like and polite. The more rigorous [4] ones simply said she was dull, plain and irresponsive. [5] However, no one knew that she was shy, uncomfortably, painfully shy.

As the years passed Doctor Sloper, who was a philosopher, got used to his disappointment. "I expect nothing from her," he said to himself. "If she gives me a surprise, I will be happy. If she doesn't, I will not lose anything."

---

1. **docile** : quiet and easy to control.
2. **affectionate** : showing gentle love.
3. **ashamed of** : embarrassed about.
4. **rigorous** : strict.
5. **irresponsive** : not reacting quickly.

Listening

1 Listen carefully to the reading of the first chapter, then decide whether the following statements are true (T) or false (F). Then correct the false ones.

		T	F
a.	Doctor Sloper lived in Washington.	☐	☐
b.	His prescriptions were illegible.	☐	☐
c.	Doctor Sloper was not interested in his wife's money.	☐	☐
d.	Everybody criticized Doctor Sloper for his wife's and son's deaths.	☐	☐
e.	Lavinia Penniman was Doctor Sloper's favourite sister.	☐	☐
f.	Doctor Sloper wanted his daughter to be, above all, a good woman.	☐	☐
g.	Mrs Penniman had never had a lover.	☐	☐
h.	Catherine had inherited her mother's beauty.	☐	☐
i.	Doctor Sloper couldn't be proud of his daughter.	☐	☐
j.	Catherine was plain but she was lady-like and polite.	☐	☐

Comprehension and personal response

2 Answer the following questions.

a. What kind of person does Doctor Sloper seem to be? Can you imagine what he must have looked like?

b. Do you think he is pleased with his daughter?

c. How would you describe Catherine? What do you think her relationship with her father was like?

d. Scan the text and find the adjectives that describe the characters that you have met in this chapter and put them in the right list:

Catherine ....

Doctor Sloper ....

Mrs Penniman ....

Antonyms

3 Find the opposites of the following words. If you consider them carefully you will find that some pairs are already present. Use a dictionary to help you.

honest ....bright...

honourable...............................charming ....

beautiful...................................shy...

successful.................................robust ....

romantic ....tall..

thin ....fair...

healthy.....................................large...

reasonable ....obedient ....

clever ....ugly ....

plain...dull...

Grammar – The Past Simple

4 Scan the text and find at least 12 regular or irregular verbs in the past. Can you complete the pattern? One has been done for you.

Infinitive	Past Simple	Past Participle
to know	knew	known
....	....	....
....	....	....
....	....	....
....	....	....
....	....	....
....	....	....

CHAPTER 2

An Important Encounter

hen Catherine finally realised that she was becoming a young lady, she tried to compensate for [1] her lack of eloquence [2] and attractiveness by wearing elaborate clothes. These clothes were expensive and brightly coloured but totally lacked class [3] and elegance.

Doctor Sloper hated vulgarity [4] and liked simple, elegant things. The thought that his daughter was both ugly and overdressed [5] irritated him immensely.

When Catherine was twenty years old she bought herself a red and gold evening dress, which she had secretly desired for many years. This evening dress made her look like a woman of thirty.

---

1. **compensate for** : make up for.
2. **eloquence** : ability to express ideas and opinions well.
3. **class** : elegance.
4. **vulgarity** : lack of good taste or refinement.
5. **overdressed** : dressed more formally or richly than is suitable for the occasion.

21

It must be added that one day Catherine would become a very rich woman. For a long time Doctor Sloper had been making twenty thousand dollars a year and saving half of it. Catherine would one day inherit [1] this fortune.

Some three or four years before this, in 1835, Doctor Sloper had decided to move his family to a quieter and more fashionable address so he built a handsome, modern house with a big balcony in Washington Square, next to Fifth Avenue. In front of the house was the square with a garden.

Mrs Almond lived out of the city near the country, where life still had a rural flavour. She had nine children, seven boys and two girls. Catherine visited her cousins every week. Now the young Almonds were growing up and the boys were either working or studying at college, while the girls were looking for appropriate husbands.

When Marian Almond, a pretty girl of seventeen, became engaged to a promising boy of twenty, Mrs Almond gave a party to celebrate the event.

Catherine, who was now twenty-one, was obviously invited. She was unaware [2] that this was the beginning of something important in her life. Catherine arrived at the party with her aunt, Mrs Penniman. Shortly after the dancing had started, Marian Almond came up to Catherine and introduced her to a tall young man. She told Catherine that the young man had a great desire to meet her. He was a cousin of Arthur Townsend, her fiancé.

---

1. **inherit** : receive money or property from someone who has died.
2. **unaware** : having no knowledge, ignorant.

An Important Encounter

Catherine was very ill at ease [1] when meeting a new person. She did not know what to say or do. Morris Townsend, the young man, immediately smiled and started talking to her.

"What a delightful party! What a charming house! What an interesting family! What a pretty girl your cousin is!"

As Morris Townsend talked, he looked straight into Catherine's eyes. She answered nothing; she only listened and looked at him. He continued to say many other things in a very easy, comfortable manner. It seemed natural that such a handsome young man should talk while she looked at him and listened silently.

He smiled and asked her to dance when the music began to play again. She gave no answer but let him put his arm around her and he guided her around the room to the music of a polka. [2]

When they paused Catherine's face was red. "Does dancing make you dizzy?" [3]

"Yes," she said, although she did not know why, since dancing had never made her dizzy.

"In that case, we will sit and talk. I will find a good place to sit," said Mr Townsend.

He found a good place—a charming place; a little sofa for two people.

"*We* will talk," the young man had said, but he still did all the talking. Catherine sat in her place with her eyes fixed upon

---

1. **ill at ease** : uncomfortable, nervous.
2. **polka** : a fast lively dance.
3. **dizzy** : light-headed, confused.

him, smiling, thinking he was very clever and admiring his delicate features. [1] He was tall and slim, but he looked very strong. She had never seen such a handsome young man and thought he looked like a statue.

Morris Townsend told her that he was Arthur Townsend's distant cousin. Although he was a native of New York, he was a stranger there since he had been away for many years. He had travelled around the world, living in strange places, and now he felt lonely.

"You see, people forget you," he said, smiling at Catherine with his delightful gaze. [2]

It seemed to Catherine that no one who had seen him would ever forget him, but she kept this reflection [3] to herself.

Catherine was completely absorbed [4] by Morris Townsend. He was very amusing and she had never heard anyone speak as well as he did. It was the way a young man might talk in a novel or in a play at the theatre. And yet, Mr Townsend was not like an actor; he seemed so sincere, so natural.

All of a sudden Marian Almond came pushing through the crowd and gave a little cry when she found the young people still together, which made Catherine blush. Marian told Mr Townsend that her mother wanted to introduce him to Mr Almond.

"We shall meet again," he said to Catherine, as he left her, and she thought it was a very original speech.

---

1. **features** : eyes, nose, mouth and other parts of the face.
2. **gaze** : steady, fixed look.
3. **reflection** : thought.
4. **absorbed** : with somebody's attention completely attracted by something.

Comprehension and personal response

1 **Answer the following questions.**

a. Explain in your own words why Catherine liked to wear showy clothes.

b. Can you describe Morris Townsend? Find the adjectives used in the text and put them in the right column.

Physical aspect	Character
....	....
....	....
....	....

c. Do you think Catherine is attracted to him? What makes you think so? Support your deductions quoting passages from the chapter.

d. Try to imagine Catherine's thoughts about Morris Townsend at the party, and write them down.

e. Now do the same with Morris's thoughts.

Listening

2 **Listen to the CD from "When Catherine finally..." to "... to celebrate the event". While you listen, write down the words or phrases that mean:**

a. as the last of a series of things

....

b. wearing clothes too rich or showy

....

c. a kind of garment women wear at parties

....

d. not spending, keeping

....

e. to go to live in a different place

....

f. it was almost like living in the country

....

g. right or suitable

....

h. agreed to marry

....

Grammar

3 **Here are examples of the Past Perfect taken from the text:**
– *he had been away for many years*
– *he had travelled around the world*

Now complete the following sentences using the words in brackets.

a. I liked that drink. I .... it before. *(never try)*

b. He wasn't hungry because he .... something to eat. *(already have)*

c. When we met them they told us they .... from India. *(just come back)*

d. When the Smiths arrived at the airport their plane .... *(already leave)*

e. When she arrived at the office, her boss .... *(already go out)*

CHAPTER 3

New Feelings

Marian Almond took Catherine by the arm and asked, "What do you think of Morris?"

"Oh, nothing particular," Catherine answered, hiding her true feelings for the first time in her life.

"I think I'll tell him that!" cried Marian. "It will do him good; he's so terribly conceited." [1]

"Conceited?" said Catherine, staring.

"So Arthur says, and Arthur knows him."

"Oh, don't tell him!" Catherine murmured imploringly. [2]

"Don't tell him he's conceited! I have told him so a dozen times."

Catherine was amazed at her cousin's audacity. [3] Half an

---

1. **conceited** : too proud of yourself.
2. **imploringly** : earnestly.
3. **audacity** : daring, bravery.

New Feelings

hour later she saw her Aunt Penniman sitting and talking with Morris Townsend. Mrs Penniman was smiling as if she approved of what Morris Townsend was saying.

Catherine moved away because she did not want to be seen by her aunt and Morris. The whole thing gave her pleasure.

One of the Almond boys invited Catherine to dance a quadrille, [1] which kept her feet busy for a quarter of an hour. This time she was not dizzy.

After the dance, she found herself face to face with her father, who had his usual little smile. He looked at his daughter's red and gold evening dress.

"Is this magnificent person my child?" he said. He almost always addressed his daughter ironically. [2] Catherine never fully understood the hidden meanings of his words, but felt they were valuable and wise.

"I am not magnificent," she said, wishing she had put on another dress.

"You are opulent, [3] expensive," her father said. "You look as if you had $80,000 a year!"

As they drove home in the carriage, [4] Doctor Sloper talked with his sister.

"Who was the young man you talked with for so long? He seemed so devoted to you."

"He was not devoted to me; he was devoted to Catherine."

---

1. **quadrille** : dance in which the dancers form a square.
2. **ironically** : in a way that means the opposite of what you say.
3. **opulent** : having signs of great wealth.
4. **carriage** :

Catherine, who had been listening attentively, exclaimed, "Oh, Aunt Penniman!" She was thankful it was dark inside the carriage.

"He is very handsome, clever and charming," her aunt continued. "He is in love with this regal [1] creature, then?" the Doctor asked

---

1. **regal** : of or like a queen.

humorously.

"Oh, father!" cried Catherine softly; thankful that the carriage was dark.

"I don't know that, but he admired her dress," said Aunt Penniman.

Admiring the dress instead of the person might not have been much of a compliment [1] for most young girls, but Catherine was very pleased.

Doctor Sloper looked at her expensive evening dress with a cool smile and said, "You see, he thinks you have $80,000 a year."

"I don't believe he thinks of that," said Mrs Penniman. "He is too refined." [2]

"He must be tremendously refined not to think of that," replied the Doctor.

"Well, he is!" Catherine exclaimed, before she knew it.

"I thought you were sleeping," her father answered.

Then he said to himself, "The hour has come! Lavinia is going to arrange a romance for Catherine. It's a shame [3] to play with the girl's feelings."

---

1. **compliment** : praise.
2. **refined** : elegant.
3. **a shame** : *(here)* wrong.

Comprehension and personal response

1 **Answer the following questions.**

    a. Who did Catherine dance the quadrille with? Why do you think this time she didn't got dizzy?

    b. Does Aunt Penniman approve of Morris Townsend? What are the adjectives she uses to describe him?

    c. Is Doctor Sloper pleased that a young man has noticed his daughter? Why does he think Morris liked Catherine's dress?

    d. How does Catherine reveal her feelings about Morris?

Words

2 **Scan the text and find the meaning of the words:**

    a. having too high an opinion of one's own ability or value. (*adj.*)

    b. very surprised (*adj.*)

    c. beautiful, impressive (*adj.*)

    d. rich, highly decorated (*adj.*)

    e. vehicle with four wheels, pulled by a horse or horses once used to carry people (*n.*)

    f. polite, well educated or belonging to a high social class (*adj.*)

    g. a love story (*n.*)

Looking back

3 **Reread this chapter and rearrange the following sentences in the correct order.**

a. Catherine danced a quadrille while Morris was talking to her aunt.

b. Doctor Sloper thought that his sister was going to arrange a romance for Catherine.

c. Marian Almond told Catherine that Morris was very conceited.

d. Doctor Sloper said that Morris probably thought that Catherine had $80,000 a year because she was wearing an expensive-looking dress.

e. Doctor Sloper told his daughter that she looked opulent.

f. Aunt Penniman said Morris was too refined to think of Catherine's money.

g. While they were driving home in the carriage, Doctor Sloper asked his sister about the young man she had been talking to.

Grammar

4 **You use reported speech to refer to something that has been said, asked or ordered usually by somebody else. Remember that when we go from direct to reported speech, changes take place.**

Now change the following sentences, adapted from the text, into reported speech.

a. Marian Almond asked Catherine, "What do you think of Morris?"

b. "Oh, don't tell him!" Catherine implored her cousin.

c. "Is this magnificent person my child?" he asked.

d. Doctor Sloper asked his sister, "Who was the young man you talked with for so long?"

e. "He is very handsome, clever and charming," her aunt declared.

f. "I don't believe he thinks of that," said Mrs Penniman.

g. Doctor Sloper thought, "The hour has come!"

CHAPTER 4

A Late Autumn Afternoon

few days after the Almond party, Morris Townsend and his cousin Arthur called at Washington Square. Catherine and her aunt were sitting by the fire in the parlour. [1] It was a late Sunday afternoon in autumn.

Arthur Townsend sat by Catherine and proudly talked to her about his new home, since he was getting married soon.

Morris Townsend sat next to Aunt Penniman and began conversing [2] with her. Catherine was usually easy to please, but this evening she found Arthur rather uninteresting. She kept

---

1. **parlour** : room in a private house used by the family for receiving guests.
2. **conversing** : talking.

looking over at the other side of the room and was listening to what Mr Townsend and her aunt were saying. She was a little envious [1] of Aunt Lavinia who sat next to Morris enjoying his company.

Arthur noticed that Catherine was interested in his cousin. "My cousin asked me to bring him," he explained. "He said Mrs Penniman had invited him."

"We are very glad to see him," said Catherine. Although she wanted to talk more about him, she did not know what to say. "I never saw him before," she went on.

Arthur Townsend stared. "But he told me he talked with you for over half an hour the other night."

"I mean before the other night. That was the first time."

"Oh, he has been away from New York—he has been all around the world."

"My aunt likes him very much," said Catherine.

"Most people like him—he's so brilliant," added Arthur.

"He's more like a foreigner," Catherine suggested.

"Well, I never knew a foreigner," said Arthur Townsend.

"Neither have I," Catherine confessed, "but people say they are generally brilliant."

"Well, the people of the city are clever enough for me."

"I suppose you can't be too clever," said Catherine with humility. [2]

---

1. **envious** : jealous.
2. **humility** : the quality of being humble.

"Well, some people say that my cousin is too clever."

Catherine listened with extreme interest. If Morris Townsend had a fault, [1] it would naturally be that one, she thought.

"Now that he has come back, will he stay here always?"

"Ah, if he can find something to do," answered Arthur. "He's looking around for some kind of employment [2] or business, but he can't find anything."

"I am very sorry," said Catherine quickly.

"Oh, he doesn't mind," Arthur said. "He isn't in a hurry."

"Won't his father take him into his business—his office?" Catherine asked.

"He hasn't got a father—he has only got a sister."

Arthur looked across to his cousin and began laughing, "We're talking about you."

Morris smiled and stood up, "I'm afraid I'm not talking about you, Arthur. However, I can't say that we didn't talk about Miss Sloper."

Catherine thought that this was a wonderfully clever thing to say but she was embarrassed by it.

"I will tell her what you have said when you go," said Aunt Penniman. Catherine blushed and almost felt that they were making fun of her; then she stood up.

Morris Townsend stood looking at her and smiling; he put out his hand to say goodbye. "I haven't talked with you and that was

---

1. **fault** : imperfection, defect.
2. **employment** : occupation.

what I came for. But it is a good reason for coming another time."

When the two men left, Catherine was still blushing when she asked her aunt, "What did you say you would tell me?"

Mrs Penniman smiled, looked at her, fixed her ribbon and nodded, "It's a great secret, my dear child, but he is coming here to court [1] you!"

Catherine was silent. "Is that what he told you?"

"He didn't say so exactly; but he left me to guess it. I'm good at guessing." Mrs Penniman gave her niece a delicate little kiss. "You must be very gracious [2] to him."

Catherine was amazed, "I don't understand you. He doesn't know me."

"Oh yes, he does; more than you think. I have told him all about you," Aunt Penniman said.

"Oh, Aunt Penniman," murmured Catherine, "He is a stranger—we don't know him."

Aunt Penniman then spoke with a touch of [3] harshness, [4] "My dear Catherine, you know very well that you admire him."

"Oh, Aunt Penniman," Catherine murmured again. Perhaps she did admire him, though this did not seem to her a thing to talk about. But she simply could not believe that this brilliant stranger wanted to court her. Only a romantic woman with a great imagination, like Aunt Lavinia, would believe that.

---

1. **court** : pay amorous attention to someone with the hope of marrying her.
2. **gracious** : kind or polite.
3. **a touch of** : a small amount of something.
4. **harshness** : severity.

Comprehension and personal response

1 **Answer the following questions.**

    a. Who is Arthur Townsend? What kind of person is he? Among the adjectives given below pick those you think describe him best.

> **brilliant   smug   self-confident   clever   rough**
>
> **inquisitive   superficial   open   simple   arrogant**

    b. Find the sentences that give you an idea of Morris's social and financial situation.

    c. Why do you think Morris only talks to Aunt Lavinia during the visit?

    d. Find Morris's sentence that indirectly means "We were talking about Catherine".

    e. Read the following sentences and choose the best description of Catherine's feelings at this stage of the story:

        i. I don't know him well yet, but he is so clever and attractive that I can't believe he is interested in me.

        ii. He is like a foreigner and he is too clever: I don't think I should encourage a stranger.

        iii. He is very attractive, but if he doesn't find some kind of employment, I'm afraid he will soon leave New York again and I want him to stay.

Words

2 **a.** Check in your dictionary the meanings of the verb "call" and try to find "call at". What does it mean?

    b. Now try to find a few other ways of saying it.

Grammar

3 Reread the text and find the *-ing* form sentences that you can list under the following headings.

Present Progressive	Future	Past Progressive
....	....	....
....	....	....
....	....	....
....	....	....
....	....	....
....	....	....
....	....	....

Food for thought

4 Do people "visit" nowadays the way they used to? Try to explain the differences in social intercourse between our society and the society James describes.

....
....
....
....
....
....
....

CHAPTER 5

A Surprise Visit

D octor Sloper came into the parlour half an hour later.

"He has just visited us, Austin. What a pity you missed him!" Aunt Penniman exclaimed.

"Who have I missed?" asked Doctor Sloper.

"Mr Morris Townsend, the gentleman at Elizabeth's party who was so impressed with Catherine," Mrs Penniman added.

"Oh, his name is Morris Townsend, is it?" the Doctor said. "And did he come here to propose [1] to you, Catherine?"

"Oh, father," murmured Catherine, turning towards the window.

"I hope he won't do that without your permission," said Mrs Penniman graciously.

---

1. **propose** : offer marriage.

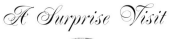

"After all, my dear, he seems to have yours," her brother answered. "The next time he comes, you should call me. He might like to see me."

Morris Townsend came again about five days later, but Doctor Sloper was away from home at that time. Catherine was with her aunt when the servant announced the young man.

"This time it's for you—for you only," Aunt Penniman said.

So Catherine saw Morris Townsend alone and the visit was a long one. He seemed more at ease [1] this time, he was more familiar with the surroundings, which he observed carefully. When he talked to her it made her think of a knight in a poem. His eyes were solemnly beautiful, Catherine thought.

"Tell me about yourself; give me a little sketch," [2] Morris said.

Catherine had very little to tell and she had no talent for sketching. However, she told him of her passion for the theatre and her love for operatic music—that of Bellini and Donizetti in particular. She also confessed that she was not fond of literature.

Morris Townsend agreed with her that books were boring. He had been to places that he had read about, and they were not at all like the descriptions. During his travels he had also seen important actors in the best theatres in London and Paris. But

---

1. **at ease** : relaxed, comfortable.
2. **sketch** : (here) short description in words.

the actors were like the authors—they always exaggerated. He liked everything to be natural. Suddenly he stopped and looked at Catherine with his smile. "That's why I like you; you are so natural. You see I am natural myself."

He began talking about music and said it was his great pleasure in life. "I sing a little myself," he said. "Some day I will show you. Not today, but some other time."

He got up to go. Catherine could only think that "some other time" had a delightful sound; it seemed to indicate other meetings in the future.

Catherine felt obliged to tell her father about Morris Townsend's visit. She announced the fact very suddenly and tried to leave the room quickly. Her father stopped her as she reached the door.

"Well, my dear, did he propose to you today?"

Catherine didn't like his comment, it made her unhappy. She wanted to give a clever answer, but she only stood by the door and gave a little laugh,

The Doctor said to himself, "My daughter is definitely not brilliant!"

But no sooner had he made this reflection, than Catherine found something to say, "Perhaps he will do it next time," and gave a repetition of her laugh, as she quickly left the room.

Comprehension and personal response

1 **Answer the following questions.**

   a. Did Doctor Sloper meet Morris Townsend? Was he upset by
   Morris's visit?

   b. Did Morris take a long time to visit Catherine again?

   c. Read carefully the dialogue between Catherine and Morris and
   write down what they like and what they dislike:

	Catherine	Morris
likes	....	....
dislikes	....	....

   d. Do you think Catherine wanted to see Morris again? Find the
   passage that makes you think so.

   e. Was Catherine pleased to have to tell her father about Morris's
   visit? Why?/Why not?

Words

2 **a.** Look up the word "parlour" in your dictionary and find one or
   more synonyms for it.
   Have we got "parlours" in our houses nowadays? What have we
   got instead?
   What is an "ice cream parlour" ? And a "beauty parlour"?

   b. Find the meaning of the verb "propose" and then rewrite Doctor
   Sloper's question ("Well, my dear, did he propose to you today?")

Listening

3 Without looking back at the text, try to decide which of these statements are true (T) and which are false (F). If you are in doubt, write "not sure". Then listen to the CD and check your answers. Correct the false ones.

		T	F
a.	Doctor Sloper's first name was Augustine.	☐	☐
b.	Morris Townsend was not very relaxed.	☐	☐
c.	Catherine thought Morris's eyes were like those of a knight in a poem.	☐	☐
d.	Morris found books boring.	☐	☐
e.	Morris had a good voice.	☐	☐
f.	Catherine's answer left her father puzzled.	☐	☐

CHAPTER 6

An Important Dinner

After his talk with Catherine the Doctor wondered whether she was serious, and he decided to find out much more about this handsome young man. He addressed himself to Mrs Almond.

"Lavinia has already asked me about him," Mrs Almond said. "She is strangely excited."

"Well, what did you tell her?" the Doctor asked.

"What I tell you—that I know very little of him."

"Lavinia must have been disappointed," said the Doctor. "She would prefer him to have some romantic secret in his life. He is a distant cousin of Arthur Townsend, isn't he?"

"Yes, but there are Townsends and Townsends—some are better than others. Arthur's mother knows very little about him.

She has only a vague [1] story that he has been "wild" in the past.
I know his sister a little, a very nice woman. Her name is Mrs
Montgomery, a widow with a little property and with five
children."

"What is his profession?" asked the Doctor.

"He hasn't got any; he is looking for something. I think he
was once in the Navy." [2]

"Once? How old is he?"

"I suppose he's more than thirty. Arthur told me he inherited
a little money which was perhaps why he left the Navy—and he
spent it all in a few years. He travelled all over the world, lived
abroad and amused himself. He has recently come back to
America to start a new life!"

"Is he serious about Catherine?"

"I don't see why you are surprised," said Mrs Almond. "It
seems to me that you have never been fair to Catherine. You
must remember that one day she will have $30,000 a year."

The Doctor looked at his sister for a moment, and then, with
a touch of bitterness [3] said, "I see that you remember it."

Mrs Almond blushed. "I don't mean that this is her only
merit. [4] I simply mean that it is a great one. A great many men
think so. You have always thought that nobody will ever want to
marry Catherine."

---

1. **vague** : not clearly expressed.
2. **Navy** : the part of a country's armed forces which operates at sea.
3. **bitterness** : anger, hostility.
4. **merit** : excellence.

An Important Dinner

"How can I think differently," asked the Doctor, "How many young men have courted Catherine, with her great fortune? How much attention has she received? None! Catherine is completely unattractive. Why do you think Lavinia is so excited that there is a lover in the house? There has never been one before! Young men prefer pretty, lively girls. Catherine is neither pretty nor lively."

"Catherine has her own style. I think young men are rather afraid of her. She is so large and she dresses so richly. She looks older than they are. Young men marry so young—before twenty-five, at the age of innocence and sincerity—before the age of calculation. [1] An older, more experienced man would certainly recognise and appreciate the good things in her character. Wait until some intelligent man of forty comes along; he will be delighted with Catherine," Mrs Almond said.

"And Mr Townsend? What are his reasons for courting her? Is he sincere?" the Doctor asked.

"It is very possible that he is sincere. Lavinia is sure of it."

Doctor Sloper reflected for a moment. "If he does not work, how does he live?"

"I have no idea. As I said before, he lives with his sister and her children on Second Avenue."

"A widow with five children? Do you mean he lives *upon* her?"

Mrs Almond got up and with a certain impatience said, "Why don't you ask Mrs Montgomery herself."

"I may do it!" replied the Doctor as he made a note of Second Avenue.

---

1. **calculation** : selfish planning.

Doctor Sloper was more amused than annoyed that Catherine was being courted by Mr Townsend. He even promised himself some entertainment from the situation.

He was very willing [1] to give Mr Townsend the benefit of the doubt. It did not matter if he was poor, he had never planned that his daughter should marry a rich man. The fortune she

---

1. **willing** : prepared, ready.

would inherit was more than sufficient for two reasonable people. He was very curious to see if Catherine might really be loved for her moral worth. [1]

The Doctor told Mrs Penniman, "The next time Mr Townsend comes here, please invite him to dinner, along with a few other people."

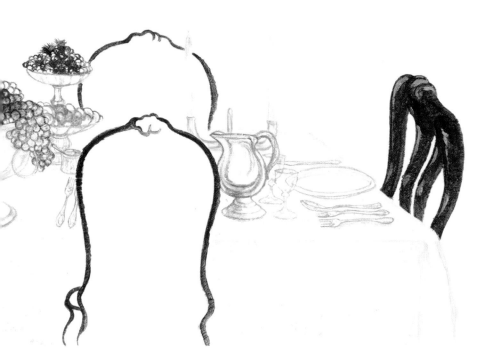

1. **worth** : value.

Washington Square

The Doctor talked to him very little during the dinner, but watched him carefully. At the end of the meal when the ladies had gone, the Doctor offered Mr Townsend some excellent wine.

As he drank, Morris thought about the attractive prospect of having a cellar [1] full of good wine.

The Doctor realised that his talkative guest was very self-confident, clever and charming with the ladies; but he did not like him. The Doctor kept these thoughts to himself.

After dinner Morris Townsend went to Catherine and said, "Your father doesn't like me—he doesn't like me at all."

"How do you know?" asked Catherine.

"I feel these things. Ask him and you will see," Morris replied.

"I would rather not, if there is any danger of his saying what you suspect."

Morris looked at her with a sad smile and said, "Wouldn't you contradict [2] him?"

"I never contradict him. But he won't say anything against you. He doesn't know you enough."

Morris laughed loudly and Catherine blushed again.

"That is fine, but I would prefer you to say that it doesn't matter what your father thinks of me."

"Ah, but it would matter! I couldn't say that," Catherine cried.

Morris looked at her and smiled a little. For a moment there was an impatient look in his eyes. He then spoke sadly, "Ah, well, I must try to make him like me."

---

1. **cellar** : underground room used for storing wine and other things.
2. **contradict** : say that a person is wrong.

An Important Dinner

The next time Doctor Sloper saw his sister Mrs Almond he told her that he had met Morris Townsend.

"He is a very handsome young man. As a doctor it is a pleasure to see such a fine specimen." [1]

"What do you think of him as a father?" asked Mrs Almond. "You know, Lavinia tells me that Catherine is in love."

"She must stop being in love! He is not a gentleman. I saw through [2] him in a minute. He is completely insincere."

"You have decided very quickly," said Mrs Almond.

"What I tell you is the result of thirty years of observation; I am able to make a judgement in a single evening."

"You may be right. But Catherine must see it."

"I will give her a pair of glasses," said the Doctor.

---

1. **specimen** : example of the human race.
2. **saw through** : understood his real nature or character.

Comprehension and personal response

1 Decide if these statements are true (T) or false (F), then correct the false ones.

		T	F
a.	Doctor Sloper decided to ask Lavinia about Morris Townsend.	☐	☐
b.	Morris's sister was a rich widow with four children.	☐	☐
c.	Morris spent all his money enjoying himself.	☐	☐
d.	Mrs Almond thought that young men were not interested in Catherine, but an older man would appreciate her character.	☐	☐
e.	Morris lived with his sister and her children.	☐	☐
f.	Doctor Sloper wanted his daughter to marry a rich man.	☐	☐
g.	Mrs Penniman invited Morris to dinner even if her brother didn't want to see him.	☐	☐
h.	Doctor Sloper watched Morris carefully and decided he didn't like him.	☐	☐
i.	Catherine told Morris it didn't matter to her if her father disliked him.	☐	☐
j.	Doctor Sloper told his sister Elizabeth he couldn't judge somebody in one evening.	☐	☐

Characters

2 a. Think about Mrs Almond. What adjectives would you use to describe her? Pick at least five among those given below.

kind   well-balanced   dull   understanding

snobbish   boring   compassionate   practical

well-informed   self-conscious   self-confident

b. Note down the following information about Morris's sister:

name	....
civil status	....
number of children	....
means of support	....
address	....

c. Why do you think Doctor Sloper decides to invite Morris to dinner?

d. Make a list of Morris's good points and bad points according to Doctor Sloper's judgment of him.

Good points	**Bad points**
....	....
....	....
....	....
....	....

Grammar

3 **Scan the passage and find the meaning of the phrasal verbs:**

a. discover ....

b. try to find ....

c. return ....

d. arrive, appear ....

e. rise ....

f. keep one's eyes in ....
a particular direction ....

g. not be deceived ....

Looking back

4 **Reread this chapter and underline the sentence or sentences that mean:**

    a. "Catherine isn't pretty and her qualities are not the kind that young men appreciate."

    b. "Your father has seen through me."

    c. "I can't push you too far, I'll wait."

5 **Match the following descriptions of Catherine with the name of the person you think would describe her so.**

    a. Not very brilliant, and hopeless in conversation but easily influenced and grateful for the attention received from a charming young man, and above all very well off!

    b. A good girl but not a brilliant one, very plain and with no taste in clothes. Not likely to attract the attention of eligible [1] young men: an easy prey to a fortune hunter.

    c. A good girl and a rich one, too; not very good looking perhaps and a bit too large, but it isn't impossible for someone to fall in love with her.

---

1. **eligible** : suitable.

CHAPTER 7

Catherine is in Love

f it were true that Catherine was in love, she was certainly very quiet about it. She had told Morris Townsend that she would not mention him to her father, and so she never mentioned his numerous visits. After the dinner at Washington Square it was only polite for Morris to visit, and the visits continued.

These visits were the most important thing in Catherine's life. She was very happy, although she did not yet know what the future would bring. She was simply grateful for the present. Morris's voice, his face, his words were always in her mind.

Catherine's father suspected Morris Townsend's visits and noticed Catherine's silence. This silence irritated the Doctor more than anything else. He hated to talk to Lavinia about this matter, since there was an air of mystery about her. But he needed to know what was happening.

One day he asked Lavinia, "What is going on in this house?"

"Going on, Austin?" exclaimed Mrs Penniman. "Well, I don't know. I think the old grey cat had kittens last night."

"At her age?" said the Doctor, as he smoked his cigar. "The idea's surprising! But what else has happened? Why haven't you told me that Morris Townsend is coming to the house four or five times a week?"

Mrs Penniman raised her eyebrows and said, "Four times a week!"

"Three times or five times, if you prefer. I am away all day and I see nothing."

With her eyebrows still raised, Mrs Penniman said, "I cannot reveal a secret."

"Whose secret? Catherine's? Mr Townsend's? If it is Mr Townsend's secret, it is very indiscreet [1] to form secret alliances [2] with young men. You don't know where they may lead you."

"I don't know what you mean by alliance," said Mrs Penniman. "I take great interest in Mr Townsend, I won't deny it. But that is all."

"That is quite enough. What is so interesting about Mr

---

1. **indiscreet** : not careful or polite in what you say or do.
2. **alliances** : agreement between people to work together and support each other.

Catherine is in Love

Townsend? His good looks?"

"His misfortunes, Austin. I don't think I can tell you his story. I am sure he would tell you if you listened kindly."

The doctor gave a laugh. "Then I shall ask him very kindly to leave Catherine alone."

"Catherine has probably said something to him kinder than that!"

"Said that she loved him?—do you mean that?"

Mrs Penniman stared at the floor and said, "She doesn't talk to me about him. All I can say is that Catherine is very happy."

"Townsend is trying to marry her—is that what you mean?"

"He is very interested in her and says charming things about her. Catherine has a lovely nature and Mr Townsend has had the intelligence to discover it."

"Do you think he is sincere?" asked her brother.

"Deeply sincere."

Doctor Sloper continued to smoke his cigar in silence. "What about the misfortunes that you haven't told me about? Did they make him poor?"

"It's not only a question of money. He is very much alone in the world. He has had false friends who have betrayed [1] him. He has been wild in the past and he has paid for it. It's a long story," said Mrs Penniman.

---

1. **betrayed** : were not loyal or faithful.

"I've heard that he lives with his sister and her children, and does nothing for himself."

"He is very seriously looking for a position."

"Precisely. He is looking for it here, over there in the front parlour. The position of husband of a weak woman with a large fortune would suit [1] him perfectly."

Mrs Penniman got up, looked at her brother angrily and said, "My dear Austin, if you think Catherine is a weak woman, then you are greatly mistaken." And with this she walked majestically [2] away.

---

1. **suit** : *(here)* satisfy, please.
2. **majestically** : in a dignified and grand way.

Comprehension and personal response

1 **Answer the following questions.**

   a. What makes Catherine happy?

   b. Does she show her feelings?

   c. What irritates Doctor Sloper?

   d. Does Aunt Penniman say that Catherine is in love?

   e. What does she think Morris appreciates in her niece?

   f. Can you list Morris's "misfortunes"?

   g. During their conversation Aunt Penniman tells her brother something unexpected about Catherine. What is it? Does it agree with the idea you had formed of Catherine's character?

Words

2 **a.** Choose among the following adjectives those that best describe Doctor Sloper:

> **bitter   intelligent   mean   superficial   suspicious disappointed   affectionate   brilliant   dull   generous deep   trusting   sweet   cold   enthusiastic   stupid**

   b. Now pair the adjectives above with their opposites.

Listening

3 **Listen to the conversation between Mrs Penniman and her brother and take notes of what she says about Morris Townsend. Then rearrange your notes into a full description of him from her point of view.**

Grammar

4 **Link the sentences below by putting one of the words from the box in each empty space.**

> **because**   **as**   **therefore**   **so**   **unless**   **as a result**

a. Catherine was in love, ... she was very happy.

b. .... Doctor Sloper didn't know what was going on, he had to ask his sister Lavinia.

c. .... of his misfortunes, Morris had become poor.

d. Morris Townsend was looking for a position .... he had lost all his money.

e. The two young people could not marry .... the girl's father gave his consent.

f. Mrs Penniman was angry with her brother, ... she left the room.

CHAPTER 8

Morris Townsend and the Doctor

I t was customary [1] for the family in Washington Square to spend Sunday evening at the Almond's house. On the Sunday after his conversation with Mrs Penniman, the Doctor spoke with his brother-in-law about a business matter.

When he returned to the large sitting room, he found Morris Townsend sitting on a small sofa beside Catherine. There were many people in the room and it was easy for the two young people to talk privately. Doctor Sloper noticed immediately that his daughter was painfully conscious that he was watching her.

---

1. **customary** : usual.

She sat motionless, [1] her eyes down, blushing deeply.

The Doctor almost pitied her. "Poor Catherine," he thought, "it must be so satisfying for a plain, inanimate [2] girl to have such a handsome young man court her. Perhaps I am condemning Morris Townsend without a reason. I should give him another chance."

Doctor Sloper crossed the room and saw Morris Townsend at the fireplace. The young man looked at him with a little smile.

"He's amazingly conceited," thought the Doctor. Then he said, "I am told you are looking for a position."

"Yes, I would like to find some work, but I have no special talents."

"You are too modest," said the Doctor. "I know nothing of you, but I see by your face that you are extremely intelligent."

"Oh," Townsend said, "I don't know what to answer when you say that. Then, do you advise me not to give up hope?"

The question seemed to have a double meaning. The Doctor observed him a moment before answering. "A young man should never give up hope. If he doesn't succeed in one thing he can try another."

Morris Townsend looked down at his remarkably neat shoes. He then looked up, smiled and asked, "Were you kindly suggesting a position for me?"

This question annoyed [3] the Doctor, who paused for a moment. "Sometimes I hear of possibilities. For example, how

---

1. **motionless** : not moving.
2. **inanimate** : dull.
3. **annoyed** : made someboby quite angry.

would you feel about leaving New York?"

"Oh, I'm afraid I could not. I must find my fortune in New York. I have responsibilities here. My sister, a widow, and her children live here. She depends on me."

"Ah, that's very proper;[1] family feeling is very important. There isn't enough of it in our city. I think I have heard of your sister."

"It is possible, but I doubt it because she lives very quietly."

"You mean as quietly as a lady may with several young children."

"Ah, yes, my nieces and nephews. I am their teacher."

"That is very good, but it isn't a career."

"It won't make my fortune," agreed the young man.

Before leaving the Almond's house, the Doctor spoke to his sister, Elizabeth.

"I should like to see his sister, Mrs Montgomery, and have a talk with her. And I should like to see the children. Mr Townsend says he teaches the children."

"I will try and arrange it," Mrs Almond answered. "He doesn't look like a school teacher, does he?"

Morris Townsend went to speak to Catherine again.

"Will you meet me somewhere tomorrow," he murmured. "I have something particular to say to you—very particular."

"Meet you?" Catherine asked, lifting her frightened eyes. "Can't you come to the house? Can't you say it there?"

---

1. **proper** : correct, right.

Morris Townsend and the Doctor

Townsend shook his head sadly. "I cannot enter your house again. Your father has insulted me."

"Insulted you?"

"He dislikes me because I am poor."

"Oh, no, you are wrong. You misunderstood him," Catherine said energetically, [1] getting up from her chair.

"Perhaps I am too proud," said Townsend.

"You must not be too proud. My father is full of goodness."

"I will only be proud of you, my dearest," said Morris and Catherine blushed. "Will you meet me in the garden in the Square in the afternoon? It is very quiet there—no one will see us."

"You know how little there is in me to be proud of. I am ugly and stupid," Catherine answered. Morris answered with a murmur, in which she recognised nothing articulate, [2] but an assurance [3] that she was his own dearest. She continued, "And I am not even brave."

"Then what shall we do if you are afraid?" asked Morris.

Catherine hesitated and at last said, "You must come to the house. I am not afraid of that."

"I would rather meet in the Square. You know how empty it is. No one will see us."

"I don't care who sees us. But leave me now."

He left her; he had got what he wanted.

---

1. **energetically** : with great effort.
2. **articulate** : clearly expressed.
3. **assurance** : confidence.

Comprehension and personal response

1 **Answer the following questions.**

   a. Find the passage where Doctor Sloper shows some fatherly affection.

   b. Doctor Sloper says that Morris is "extremely intelligent". Does it really sound like a compliment? Try to decide what the meaning of his words could be:

      i. "Even if I don't like you, I must admit that you are intelligent."

      ii. "You are using your intelligence to get a rich wife."

      iii. "I don't like people who are too intelligent."

   c. Think about Morris's question to Doctor Sloper: "Then, do you advise me not to give up hope?" What other meaning can this question have? Express it in your own words.

   d. Who does Doctor Sloper want to contact? What does he want to check?

Words

2 **Find definitions for the following adjectives:**

   a. ugly   ....   **e.** poor   ....

   b. brave   ....   **f.** handsome.............................

   c. stupid   ....   **g.** proud   ....

   d. inanimate.............................

Now match them with their synonyms:

> **good-looking**   **dumb**   **haughty**   **penniless**
>   **fearless**   **lifeless**   **unattractive**

Listening

3 **Listen to the conversation between Morris and Doctor Sloper from: "Doctor Sloper crossed the room..." to: "...agreed the young man." As you listen, complete the following parts:**

a. "I .... you are looking for a position."

b. "Yes, I .... some work, but I have no special talents."

c. "I don't know what to answer when you say that. Then, do you advise me .... hope?"

d. "Sometimes I hear of possibilities. For example, ... about leaving New York?"

e. "It is possible, but .... because she lives very quietly."

f. "That is very good but ...."

Grammar

4 **Fill in the blanks with the appropriate modal verbs.**

a. Doctor Sloper thought it .... be satisfying for his daughter to be courted by a handsome young man.

b. Morris thought Doctor Sloper .... find him a position.

c. Morris said he .... not leave New York.

d. Catherine thought Morris .... not be too proud.

CHAPTER 9

The Proposal

Catherine received the young man the next day on the ground she had chosen—in her elegantly furnished New York parlour. Mrs Penniman, who considered the situation a romantic drama that was taking place before her eyes, left the two young people alone during their meeting.

"We must decide what to do," said Morris Townsend, looking at himself in the mirror. "We must settle this."

Morris had already told Catherine that he loved her, or rather adored her. He had put his arm around her and kissed her. Catherine had felt immensely happy, but also a bit frightened and confused. After Morris had kissed her on this last visit, she had asked him to go away so that she could meditate. She had felt his kisses on her lips and her cheeks for a long time afterward, and this confused her thinking. She worried that her father would not like Morris Townsend. The thought of a conflict between her father and Morris made her heart beat, and it was painful.

Today when the young man spoke about deciding something, she felt it was the truth and said very simply, "We must do our duty. [1] We must speak to my father. I will do it tonight and you must do it tomorrow."

"It is very good of you to do it first," Morris said. "The young man—the happy lover—usually does that."

It pleased Catherine to think that she would be brave for him, and in her situation she gave a little smile. "Women have more tact. [2] They can persuade better."

"You will need all your powers of persuasion. [3] But, after all, you are irresistible," Morris said.

"Promise me this: When you talk to my father tomorrow you must be gentle and respectful."

"I shall try. But do you know what your father will say about me? He will tell you that I am a mercenary." [4]

"Mercenary!" exclaimed Catherine.

"It means that I only want your money."

"Oh," murmured Catherine softly.

Morris gave her a little kiss.

"I shall tell him he is wrong. Other men may be that way, but

---

1. **duty** : what one must do because it is right.
2. **tact** : the ability to deal with people without offending or upsetting them.
3. **persuasion** : causing somebody to do something by giving him good reasons.
4. **mercenary** : person interested only in making money.

not you."

"He will argue with you."

Catherine looked at her lover for a minute and then said, "I shall persuade him. But I am glad we shall be rich."

Morris turned away, looking down at this hat, "No, it's a misfortune. Our problems will come from that."

"Well, we are not so unhappy. I will persuade him and after that we shall be very glad we have money."

Morris listened to this robust [1] logic in silence and looked outside the window. "I will leave my defence to you."

"Morris," she said suddenly, "are you very sure you love me?"

He turned around and in a moment he was at her side. "My own dearest, can you doubt it?"

"I have only known it five days," she said, "but now it seems to me something I could not live without."

"You will never have to try," Morris said, giving a little laugh. Then he added, "There is something you must tell me, too." Catherine had closed her eyes and kept them closed. "You must tell me," Morris went on, "that if your father forbids [2] our marriage, you will still be faithful."

Catherine opened her eyes, gazed at him and she could give no better promise than what he read there.

Catherine listened for her father when he came in that

---

1. **robust** : forceful and effective.
2. **forbids** : does not allow.

The Proposal

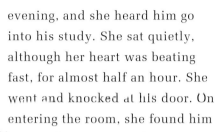

evening, and she heard him go into his study. She sat quietly, although her heart was beating fast, for almost half an hour. She went and knocked at his door. On entering the room, she found him in his chair beside the fire, with a cigar and the evening paper.

"I have something to say to you," she began very gently. [1]

"I shall be very happy to hear it my dear," said her father.

He waited, looking at her, while she stared at the fire.

"I am engaged to be married!" Catherine finally announced.

The Doctor was startled, [2] but he did not show it.

"You are right to tell me," he said. "And who is the happy man?"

---

1. **gently** : in a kind, polite and quiet manner.
2. **startled** : surprised.

"Mr Morris Townsend." As she pronounced her lover's name Catherine looked at him. She saw his still grey eyes and his smile. She looked back at the fire; it was much warmer.

"When did this happen?" the Doctor asked.

"This afternoon—two hours ago."

"Was Mr Townsend here?"

"Yes, father, in the front parlour." She was very glad that she did not have to tell him her engagement had taken place in the garden of the Square.

"Mr Townsend should have told me first."

"He wants to tell you tomorrow."

The Doctor smoked his cigar for a while and said, "You have gone very fast."

"Yes," Catherine answered simply, "I think we have."

Her father looked at her an instant, "I'm not surprised that Mr Townsend likes you; you are so simple and so good."

"I don't know why, but he *does* like me. I am sure of that. And I like him very much."

"But you have known him a very short time, my dear."

The Proposal

"Oh," said Catherine, "it doesn't take long to like a person—once you have begun."

"You have undoubtedly observed that I have left you your liberty. [1] I have not interfered. You are no longer a little girl."

"I feel very old and very wise," said Catherine, smiling.

"I am afraid that you will soon feel older and wiser. I don't like your engagement."

"Ah," Catherine exclaimed softly, getting up from her chair.

"No, my dear. I am sorry to give you pain; but I don't like it. You should have spoken to me first."

Catherine hesitated a moment and then said, "I was afraid you wouldn't like Mr Townsend."

"You were quite right. I don't like him."

"Dear father, you don't know him," said Catherine in a timid voice.

"Very true, I don't know him intimately. [2] But I have my impression of him. You don't know him either."

"I don't know him?" she cried. "I know him better than I have ever known anyone!"

"You know a part of him—the part he has chosen to show you. But you don't know the rest!"

"The rest? I know what you mean," said Catherine remembering Morris's warning. "You mean that he is a mercenary."

---

1. **liberty** : freedom.
2. **intimately** : in a close or personal way.

Her father looked up at her with his cold, quiet, reasonable eyes.

"I am not accusing Mr Townsend of that. You are an honest, kind girl and it isn't impossible for an intelligent young man to love you. But the principal thing we know about this man is that he has led a life of dissipation [1] and has spent his own fortune. There is every reason to believe that he would spend yours, too."

There was something hopeless and oppressive [2] in arguing with her father. Her efforts made her tremble.

"That is not the only thing we know about him. He is kind, generous and true; and the fortune he spent was small," said poor Catherine with a trembling voice.

The Doctor stood up. He held her for a moment and kissed her.

"You won't think that I am cruel?" he asked.

The question scared Catherine, but she said, "No, dear father; because if you knew how I feel, you would be so kind, so gentle."

"Yes, I think I know how you feel," the Doctor said. "I will be very kind. And I will see Mr Townsend tomorrow. Meanwhile, do not tell anyone that you are engaged."

---

1. **dissipation** : the state of being given to foolish and harmful pleasures.
2. **oppressive** : causing you to feel very uncomfortable.

Comprehension and personal response

1 a. **Read the following statements and decide whether they are true (T) or false (F). Then correct the false ones.**

		T	F
a.	Mrs Penniman loved romantic drama so she listened to Catherine and Morris's conversation.	☐	☐
b.	Morris hadn't kissed Catherine yet.	☐	☐
c.	Catherine was afraid her father might not like Morris Townsend.	☐	☐
d.	Catherine said she was sure Morris was not interested in her money.	☐	☐
e.	Morris made Catherine promise she would not contradict her father.	☐	☐
f.	When Catherine went into her father's study, he was sitting at his writing desk.	☐	☐
g.	Doctor Sloper was not surprised to hear that Catherine was engaged.	☐	☐
h.	Doctor Sloper said he was sorry for Catherine but he didn't like Morris.	☐	☐
i.	Morris had spent a very large sum of money.	☐	☐
j.	Doctor Sloper asked Catherine not to tell anybody about her engagement.	☐	☐

b. **Answer the following questions.**

    a. What decision do Catherine and Morris come to?

    b. What does Morris say about Catherine's money?

    c. What is Catherine's attitude about her own money?

    d. How long has Catherine known that Morris loves her?

    e. What does Doctor Sloper accuse Morris of?

    f. What do you think Catherine's father is planning to do?

Meanings

2 **Look back at Chapter 9 and underline the sentence or sentences that have the following meaning:**

    a. Catherine felt an unpleasant emotion at the thought that her father might be against her engagement.

    b. Catherine was caught by a sudden doubt about her lover's feelings.

    c. Doctor Sloper's smile had no warmth.

    d. "The bad news I'm about to give you, will make you more mature."

    e. Catherine felt she had no hope of persuading her father.

Words

3 **a.** All the words in the spidergram refer to love and marriage. Most of them are in use nowadays but a few are old-fashioned and more often found in literature than in everyday life. Can you find them?

    b. Check the meaning of the words you are not sure of and then try to add more.

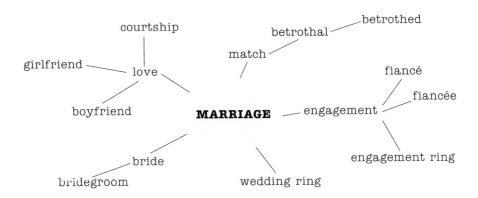

Food for thought

4 In Henry James's time, girls who wanted to marry had to have their parents' consent [1] or else they had to face the most unpleasant consequences such as being disinherited [2] and losing their parents' affection. And if their husband belonged to a lower social class, they would lose their social status, too, and with it all their former friends.

What do you think would happen to a girl in Catherine's position nowadays? Can you imagine what she would tell her father and how he would react?

---

1. **consent** : agreement, permission.
2. **disinherited** : left no money or property to a person in a will.

New York City in the 1850's

Perhaps no other city of nineteenth century America experienced the rapid growth and development of New York City. Ever since 1626, when Peter Minuit of the Dutch West India Company bought Manhattan Island (New York City) from the Indians for beads and trinkets [1] worth $24, it was destined [2] to become an international centre.

In the year 1800 the population of New York City was 60,000; by 1860 it had climbed to 800,000!

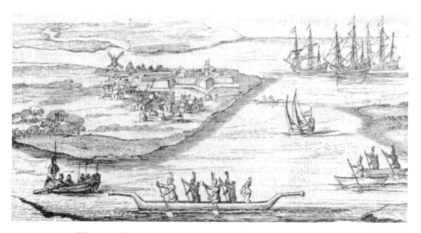

The earliest view of Manhattan about 1636-39.

---

1. **trinkets** : inexpensive pieces of jewellery.
2. **destined** : sure to be something.

In the 1850's the New York waterfront [1] was crowded with sailing ships and steamships from all over the world. Trade and commerce flourished. [2]

New York in about 1757 by an unknown artist.

The construction of the Erie Canal [3] (see map on page 80) in 1825 was a significant event for New York City. The canal was 350 miles long, from Albany to Buffalo. It connected the Hudson River to Lake Erie. Steamboats travelled on the Hudson. At Lake Erie there were railroads to the West. Goods from New York City factories were transported to

---

1. **waterfront** : part of town adjoining river, lake etc.
2. **flourished** : expanded and prospered.
3. **canal** : channel cut through land for ships to travel along.

the West quickly and cheaply. The entire region of the Great Lakes and the Midwest became an economic part of New York City: the West and the East were joined together economically. The West was a huge market.

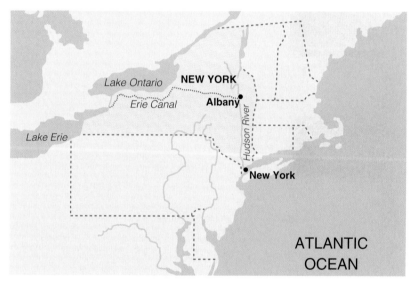

The East Coast in about 1840.

Factories, mills, [1] shipyards, [2] warehouses, offices and shops grew quickly in the southern part of the city, while elegant residential areas were born farther north of Washington Square. Industrialization was expanding, and with it the entrepreneurial [3] spirit—tenacity, [4] ambition and energy.

---

1. **mills** : where steel and textiles are made.
2. **shipyards** : where ships are built.
3. **entrepreneurial** : relating to business.
4. **tenacity** : determination.

New Yorkers, like most Americans, were very hard-working people, interested in becoming wealthy and successful. Devotion to hard work and business enterprise is the American work ethic, [1] which has become

A poster from 1860; the island of Manhattan was beginning to look like a city.

a sort of national credo. [2] Numerous fortunes were made during this period. The acquisition [3] of wealth was for most people the best way to improve their social status.

The homes, furnishings [4] and clothing of successful New Yorkers

---

1. **ethic** : belief about what is morally right and wrong.
2. **credo** : statement of beliefs and principles.
3. **acquisition** : the act of obtaining something.
4. **furnishings** : the furniture, carpets, curtains, etc in a room or house.

reflected their wealth. The Victorian style of the period became American Victorian. Homes were very richly furnished with an overwhelming [1] amount of costly furniture, curtains, Oriental rugs and other expensive accessories. [2]

A lithograph [3] from 1876 showing the crowded Erie Station in Hornellsville, New York.

During the 19th century three quarters of the immigrants that came to the United States chose New York as their city. These immigrants found work in the flourishing industries and businesses of New York

---

1. **overwhelming** : *(here)* vast.
2. **accessories** : things that are decorative but not essential.
3. **lithograph** : picture printed by lithography, a process of printing from a smooth surface treated so that ink adheres only to the design to be printed.

City, and contributed to [1] the amazing development. The majority of these immigrants came from Ireland, Germany and England. Several immigrants made their fortune in New York City: Michael Cudahy started working in a meat-packing factory at the age of fourteen and became the owner of Cudahy Packing Company; Alexander T. Stewart became the owner of America's largest department store; and Victor Herbert became one of America's famous composers.

Visitors were amazed by the latest modern improvements such as rubbish collection, sewers, [2] indoor plumbing, coal stoves and gaslights in the streets.

New Yorkers were proud of their city's commercial supremacy [3] and power!

A view of the elevated rail system, 1860.

---

1. **contributed to** : helped to produce something.
2. **sewers** : large pipes under the ground that carry water and waste material away from a city or town.
3. **supremacy** : the state of being most powerful.

1 Read the following statements and decide whether they are true
(T) or false (F). Then correct the false ones.

		T	F
a.	It took a long time for New York City to develop.	☐	☐
b.	The English West India Company bought Manhattan Island from the Indians.	☐	☐
c.	In the 1850's trade and commerce flourished.	☐	☐
d.	The southern part of New York quickly became an elegant residential area.	☐	☐
e.	New Yorkers worked hard and liked to make money.	☐	☐
f.	New Yorkers adopted the Victorian style and their houses were richly furnished.	☐	☐
g.	In the 19th century three quarters of the immigrants didn't like New York City.	☐	☐
h.	In the 19th century New York had a sewage system and gaslit streets.	☐	☐

CHAPTER 10

Doctor Sloper's Decision

The next afternoon the Doctor stayed at home and waited for Mr Townsend's visit. Morris Townsend was quite serene [1] when he arrived.

"Catherine told me yesterday what has been going on [2] between you," the Doctor said. "You should have spoken to me about your intentions before. It was only the other day that Catherine met you."

"It was not long ago, certainly," said Morris. "My interest in Miss Sloper began the first time I saw her."

"Did it not perhaps begin before you met her?" the Doctor asked.

---

1. **serene** : calm and peaceful.
2. **going on** : happening.

Morris looked at him an instant. "I had certainly already heard that she was a charming girl."

"A charming girl—that's what you think of her? As

Doctor Sloper's Decision

Catherine's father I appreciate her many good qualities, but I have never thought of her as a charming girl," said the Doctor.

"I speak from my own point of view," replied Morris.

"You speak very well," said the Doctor, "but that is not all that is necessary. I told Catherine yesterday that I do not approve of her engagement."

"She told me and I was very sorry to hear it. I am greatly disappointed," said Morris who sat in silence for a while, looking at the floor.

"Did you really expect me to say I was delighted and throw my daughter into your arms?"

"Oh, no! I had an idea that you didn't like me."

"What gave you the idea?"

"The fact that I am poor."

"It is certainly a fact I must consider. You are without a position, visible resources or prospects. You are not a suitable husband for my daughter, who is a weak young woman with a large fortune."

Morris listened respectfully. "I don't think Miss Sloper is a weak woman," he said.

"I have known my child for twenty years, and you have known her for six weeks. Even if she were not weak, you would still be a penniless [1] man."

"Yes, that is *my* weakness! You think I only want your daughter's money."

---

1. **penniless** : having no money.

"I don't say that. I simply say that you belong to the wrong category."

"But your daughter doesn't marry a category, she marries an individual," Townsend said with a handsome smile.

"An individual who offers so little in return."

"Is it possible to offer more than tender affection and life-long devotion?" the young man asked.

"Fine words," said the Doctor, "but you are still the wrong kind of man."

"You think I would spend her money, don't you?" asked Morris.

"Yes, I think you would."

Morris continued to display great self-control, although his disappointment was obvious.

"I confess that I have been wild and foolish. If you like, I will tell you every crazy thing I ever did. But I have changed now. I spent my own fortune because it was my own. That does not mean I would spend Miss Sloper's fortune. I would take good care of it."

"Taking too much care would be as bad as taking too little care. Catherine might suffer as much by your economy as by your extravagance," [1] declared the Doctor.

"I think you are very unjust," said the young man. "Do you want to make your daughter miserable?"

"She will most likely think I am cruel for a year."

---

1. **extravagance** : spending too much money.

Doctor Sloper's Decision

"A year!" exclaimed Morris with a laugh.

"For a lifetime, then. She will be miserable either way, with you or without you."

Here, at last, Morris got angry. "You are not polite, sir!" he cried.

"You argue too much. I cannot accept you as a son-in-law, and I shall advise Catherine to give you up." [1]

"Are you sure your daughter will give me up?"

"No, I am not sure of it; but I shall strongly recommend it. My daughter has a great sense of respect, affection and duty towards her father. I think it is extremely possible."

"I don't think she will—she has gone too far to stop," Morris insisted.

The Doctor looked at Morris and said, "You are very impertinent." [2]

"I will say no more, sir," said Morris, and he left the room.

---

1. **give you up** : stop having a relationship with you.
2. **impertinent** : rude.

Comprehension and personal response

1 **a.**   Is Morris Townsend nervous when he meets Catherine's father?

  b.   Doctor Sloper hints that Morris's interest may have begun before he met Catherine. What does he mean by this?

  i.   You were looking for a wife and somebody had told you that she was free.

  ii.   Somebody had told you she was rich and charming.

  iii.   Somebody had told you she was rich but plain and therefore easy to seduce.

  c.   What are Doctor Sloper's reasons for opposing the match?

  d.   "I don't think Miss Sloper is a weak woman" says Morris. We have heard these words before. Who said them? Has Catherine given any sign that these words are true yet?

  e.   What does Morris say he is offering Catherine? Do you think he means it?

  f.   How long does Catherine's father think that it will take for Catherine to forget Morris? Is this also Morris's opinion?

Words

2 **a.**   Underline the words in the text that refer directly or indirectly to money. Remember that some of them are nouns, some are adjectives and there is a verb, too.

  b.   Now make your own spidergram centred around the word "money" using the words you found in the text and adding others you can think of.

Grammar

3 "Even if she were not weak, you would still be a penniless man." This sentence from the text is in the second conditional which we use when we refer to something that is not possible in the present.

Consider the following sentences and complete them as suggested using the second conditional.

a. If Morris had a lot of money .... (*marry*) Catherine.

b. If the Slopers were not rich .... (*not live*) in Washington Square.

c. If Morris had not been foolish .... (*still have*) some money.

d. If Catherine agreed to give up Morris .... (*be*) very unhappy.

e. If Aunt Lavinia didn't like romance .... (*not help*) Morris and Catherine.

f. If Doctor Sloper loved his daughter .... (*not make*) her suffer.

Listening

4 Try and put the following sentences in the correct order without looking back at the text. Then listen to the CD from the beginning of the chapter to: "...I do not approve of her engagement" and check your answers.

a. "I had certainly heard that she was a charming girl."

b. Morris Townsend was quite serene when he arrived.

c. "I speak from my own point of view," replied Morris.

d. The Doctor said, "You should have spoken to me about your intentions before."

e. "I have never thought of her as a charming girl," said the Doctor.

f. "You speak very well," said the Doctor.

CHAPTER 11

Mrs Montgomery

he Doctor told Mrs Almond all about his meeting with Morris Townsend. She felt that he had been much too hard on the young man. The Doctor decided to give Morris the benefit of the doubt, and go and talk with his sister, Mrs Montgomery.

"She will almost certainly tell me that I have done the right thing. But it is possible that she will tell me that I have made the greatest mistake of my life. If she does, I will beg Mr Townsend's pardon."

"How is Catherine taking it?" asked Mrs Almond.

"As she takes everything—quietly, without noisy tears or anything else."

"I am very sorry for Catherine. She will have to choose between her father and her lover."

"I am sorry for her too. But she will get over [1] it."

The visit was planned for a few days later. Mrs Montgomery received the Doctor in a small front parlour of her little house

---

1. **get over** : recover from something unpleasant.

Mrs Montgomery

on Second Avenue.

She was a small, fair woman with bright, clear eyes and an air of unaffected [1] humility.

At first Mrs Montgomery was a bit unwilling [2] to talk about her brother.

"I can understand that this may be difficult for you," said the Doctor. "Please understand my situation. Your brother wishes to marry my daughter, and I wish to find out what sort of a young man he is. That is why I have come to ask you questions. Her happiness depends on whether he is a good man or not."

"Yes, I understand," murmured Mrs Montgomery.

"I must remind you that after my death Catherine will have thirty thousand dollars a year, if she marries a husband I approve."

"Your daughter will be immensely rich," she said softly.

"Precisely. But if Catherine marries without my consent, she will have only the ten thousand dollars that she inherited from her mother. She will not have a penny from me."

"Does Morris know this?" asked his sister.

"I shall be very happy to inform him!" the Doctor exclaimed.

After thinking for some time, she asked, "What makes you dislike Morris so much?"

"I don't dislike him as a friend or as a companion. He is a charming young fellow. I dislike him only as a son-in-law, whose responsibility would be to protect and take care of my child, who has difficulty taking care of herself! My daughter is weak, and not clever enough or strong enough to solve the

---

1. **unaffected** : natural.
2. **unwilling** : did not want to.

problems of life. My impression is that your brother would not be a good son-in-law. I think he is selfish and superficial. [1] Of course, you may contradict me."

Mrs Montgomery was surprised. "How did you discover that he is selfish?" she exclaimed.

"Do you think he hides it well?" asked the Doctor.

"Very well!" said Mrs Montgomery. After a brief moment of silence she said, "My brother is very handsome."

The Doctor looked at her and said, "You women are all the same! Men like your brother are the types that ruin women. They accept nothing in life but its pleasures, which they receive with the help of the gentle sex. [2] They never do anything for themselves since others do it for them. Someone else always suffers for them." The Doctor paused a moment and then added, "You have suffered immensely for your brother!"

There were now tears in Mrs Montgomery's eyes.

"Do you give your brother money?" asked the Doctor.

"Yes, I do," replied Mrs Montgomery.

"I see that I was right. Your brother lives on you, takes your money and is extremely selfish."

"But he is still my brother," she said with a trembling voice and then burst into tears.

"I am sorry that I have upset you. It's all for my poor Catherine. You must know her and you will see."

"I should like to know your daughter," she said and then, suddenly— "Don't let her marry him!"

Feeling satisfied, Doctor Sloper left with these words in his ears.

---

1. **superficial** : not caring about serious or important things.
2. **the gentle sex** : women.

Comprehension and personal response

1 **Read the following statements and decide whether they are true (T) or false (F). Then correct the false ones.**

		T	F
a.	Mrs Almond tried to soften her brother's judgment.	☐	☐
b.	Doctor Sloper was ready to apologize if he could find proof he was wrong.	☐	☐
c.	Mrs Montgomery's house on Second Avenue was very small.	☐	☐
d.	Doctor Sloper said that Catherine would find herself penniless if she decided to marry without his consent.	☐	☐
e.	Doctor Sloper liked Morris socially but not as a son-in-law.	☐	☐
f.	Mrs Montgomery denied that her brother was selfish.	☐	☐
g.	Morris used to give his sister some money.	☐	☐
h.	Doctor Sloper had been right about Morris.	☐	☐

Character

2 **a.** In your opinion which of the following explanations of Mrs Montgomery's behaviour is the correct one?

   i. She takes her revenge on her brother who leads an exciting life while she has to stay at home all the time.

   ii. She loves her brother but she is deeply honest and disapproves of his ways.

   iii. She doesn't want her brother to marry because she is alone with her five children and needs his help.

   b. Do you think Doctor Sloper's attitude is basically right or do you feel he ought to let Catherine decide for herself? Why / why not?

Words

3 **a.** Give a physical description of Mrs Montgomery. Try not to use the same words that are used in the text.

b. We only know that Mrs Montgomery's house on Second Avenue is small and has got "a small front parlour". Can you try to give a description of what the rest of the house might be like?

c. With the help of your monolingual dictionary find out the meanings of the following words and write a definition for each one of them.

Avenue ....

Street ....

Road ....

Highway ....

Toll road ....

Lane ....

Alley ....

Square ....

Circus ....

Crescent ....

Listening

4 **Try and fill in the gaps in the following paragraphs. Then listen to the CD from: "The visit was planned..." to: "a penny from me", and check your answers.**

The visit was planned for a few days later. Mrs Montgomery .... the Doctor in a small front parlour of her little house on Second Avenue.

She .... a small, fair woman with bright, clear eyes and an air of unaffected humility.

At first Mrs Montgomery .... a bit unwilling to .... about her brother.

"I .... that this .... difficult for you," .... the Doctor. "Please .... my situation. Your brother .... to .... my daughter, and I .... to .... what sort of a young man he .... That is why I .... to .... you questions. Her happiness .... on whether he .... good man or not."

"Yes, I ....," .... Mrs Montgomery.

"I .... you that after my death Catherine .... thirty thousand dollars a year, if she .... a husband I ...."

"Your daughter .... immensely rich," she .... softly.

"Precisely. But if Catherine .... without my consent, she .... only the ten thousand dollars that she .... from her mother. She .... not .... a penny from me."

CHAPTER 12

Mrs Penniman's Secret Meeting

Doctor Sloper was puzzled by the way Catherine behaved. She did not appear angry or upset—she was strangely passive. [1] She had not spoken to him again after their meeting in the library. The Doctor had probably hoped for a little more resistance on Catherine's part. It would have added a little entertainment to the dull vocation [2] of being a father.

Catherine, however, had made a discovery of a very different nature. She found that there was great excitement in trying to be a good daughter. She experienced a new feeling: suspense about her own actions. She watched herself and wondered what she

---

1. **passive** : showing no reaction or feeling.
2. **vocation** : a strong feeling that you are especially suited to fulfil a particular role in life.

Mrs Penniman's Secret Meeting

would do next. It was as if a new person had come into her life, inspiring her natural curiosity.

"I am glad I have such a good daughter," the Doctor said, after several days had passed.

"I am trying to be good," she answered, turning away.

"If you have anything to say about Mr Townsend, I shall be happy to listen."

"Thank you," said Catherine. "I have nothing particular to say at present."

He never asked her whether she had seen Morris again. She had not seen him, but she had written him a long, five-page letter in a remarkably neat and handsome handwriting. The letter, at least, was long for her, and it may be added, was also long for Morris.

"I am in great trouble," she wrote. "Do not doubt my love for you, but let me wait a while and think." She did not really believe that her father would change his mind about Morris, but she hoped that the situation would change in some mysterious way.

Poor Catherine received no help or advice from Mrs Penniman, although she would have liked some illumination [1] from her. Mrs Penniman was enjoying the sentimental drama and hoped that the plot [2] would become more complicated.

"You must act, my dear," she told Catherine. "The important thing is to act."

Mrs Penniman, who was deeply involved [3] in this situation,

---

1. **illumination** : explanation.
2. **plot** : series of events on which a story or play is based.
3. **involved** : absorbed, concerned.

wrote to Morris Townsend every day, informing him of the state of affairs [1] at Washington Square. She had even arranged a secret meeting with him in an oyster saloon [2] in the Seventh Avenue.

Morris was rather irritated as is natural for a fine gentleman who has tried to court a young woman of inferior [3] characteristics. He had made himself agreeable [4] to Mrs

---

1. **state of affairs** : events.
2. **oyster saloon** : large public drinking place where oysters are the main food.
3. **inferior** : lower in quality.
4. **agreeable** : pleasant.

Mrs Penniman's Secret Meeting

Penniman in order to get a footing [1] in Washington Square, but now he needed all his self-command [2] to be civil [3] to her.

Mrs Penniman had not told Catherine about this meeting, and when Morris arrived and asked if Catherine had sent him a message, she said, "Not exactly a message; I didn't ask her for one because I was afraid to excite her."

"I am afraid she is not very excitable," said Morris with a rather bitter smile.

"She is better than that—she is true to you until death."

"Oh, I hope it won't come to that," said Morris.

"We must be prepared for the worst," said Mrs Penniman.

"What do you mean?"

"My brother won't change his mind." There was silence for a moment, then Mrs Penniman smiled and said, "Marry Catherine first and tell him after!"

Morris stared at her and asked, "Do you advise me to marry her without her father's consent?"

Mrs Penniman was a bit frightened, but she continued, "If you marry Catherine, you will show my brother that he has been wrong about you. He will understand that it is not just because you like the... money."

Morris hesitated and then said, "But *I do* like the money."

---

1. **footing** : a secure position.
2. **self-command** : self-control.
3. **civil** : polite.

"Ah, but not more than Catherine. When he understands that, he will help you in the end."

Morris asked, "Do you think there is a will already made in Catherine's favour?"

"I suppose so—even doctors must die."

"But I can't depend on that," said Morris.

"Do you want to *depend* on it?" asked Mrs Penniman.

Morris blushed a little and said, "I do not want to injure Catherine."

"Be afraid of nothing and everything will go well!" With this, Mrs Penniman and Morris left the oyster saloon in the Seventh Avenue.

It was dark as they walked through the noisy, populous [1] streets of the west side of town to the quiet, elegant neighbourhood of Washington Square. Here they separated and Morris paused for a moment looking at Doctor Sloper's home. He thought it was a wonderfully comfortable house.

When Mrs Penniman arrived home she told Catherine about her meeting with Morris Townsend. For the first time in her life Catherine felt angry. "Why did you see him? I don't think it was right," she said.

"I was so sorry for him—you wouldn't see him," said Aunt Penniman.

---

1. **populous** : having a large population.

"I have not seen him because my father has forbidden it," Catherine said, very simply. This annoyed Mrs Penniman who began reading the evening paper. She was silent and determined that Catherine should ask her about her meeting with Morris.

After a very long silence Catherine finally spoke. "What did he say?" she asked.

"He said he is ready to marry you any day."

Catherine got up from her seat and went to the fire.

"He said he was afraid of only one thing—that you would be afraid," said Aunt Penniman.

"Afraid of what?"

"Afraid of your father."

Catherine turned back to the fire and said, "I *am* afraid of my father."

"Are you going to give him up?" asked Aunt Penniman.

Catherine kept her eyes on the fire. At last she raised her head and looked at her aunt, "Why do you push me so?" she asked. "I don't think you understand or that you know me."

"You trust me so little," said her aunt.

Catherine did not deny this and said sternly, "You had better not make any more appointments with Mr Townsend. I don't think it is right. If my father knew, he wouldn't like it."

"You will inform him—is that what you mean? I am not afraid of my brother. I have always defended my own position. I shall certainly never again try to help you because you are ungrateful. [1] I am disappointed, but your father will not be. Good night." And with this Mrs Penniman went to her room.

---

1. **ungrateful** : not showing thanks.

Comprehension and personal response

1 **Read Chapter 12 carefully and then put the following sentences in the correct sequence without looking back at the text.**

a. Catherine hadn't decided what to do yet and she hoped something would change.

b. Mrs Penniman encouraged Morris to marry Catherine without her father's consent.

c. Mrs Penniman said she would never again try to help her niece.

d. Catherine was angry because her aunt had met Morris Townsend.

e. Doctor Sloper thought that Catherine had accepted his refusal too passively.

f. Mrs Penniman arranged a meeting with Morris.

g. Catherine said her aunt did not understand her.

h. Morris said he wasn't indifferent to the money.

Character

2 **Answer the following questions.**

a. Try to give reasons why Doctor Sloper would have liked more resistance on Catherine's part.

b. "Mrs Penniman... was deeply involved in this situation." Can you explain this involvement?

c. Thinking about this and the previous chapters, what would you say is Catherine's attitude towards her father?

d. Everybody seems to want Catherine to be different from how she is. Read the following statements and match them with the character that would be most likely to say:

   i. I would like her to be less calm and self-possessed.

   ii. I would like her to be more romantic.

   iii. I would like her to be less passive.

Language production

3 Imagine Mrs Penniman is writing an account of her meeting with Morris in the oyster bar to a friend who knows the situation. You can begin like this:

Dear Arabella,

Yesterday I went to a strange part of the city (just imagine: an oyster bar in the Seventh Avenue!) to try and help the young couple because my brother is being horrid to them. They need the advice of somebody older who knows about love and suffering. Their situation is becoming more and more complicated but I am sure love will eventually triumph: that's why I advised Morris ....

....

Meanings

4 Look back at the text and try to spot the meaning of the sentences:

a. Morris had found Catherine's letter boring.

b. "She will never stop loving you."

c. He wished he could live there.

d. "Why don't you let me make my own decisions?"

CHAPTER 13

The Confrontation

atherine sat alone by the parlour fire for more than an hour.

Her aunt seemed to her aggressive [1] and foolish. She had an immense respect for her father and she felt that to displease him was a horrible thing; but her plan was slowly taking form and she had to go on with it. When the clock struck eleven, and the house was in silence, Catherine slowly went to the door of the library. She knocked and her father opened the door.

"What is the matter?" asked the Doctor. "You are standing there like a ghost!"

She went into the room but it was some time before she began to speak. Her father went back to his writing desk, sat down and

---

1. **aggressive** : ready to fight or argue.

began writing. His back was turned to her and she heard the scratching [1] of his pen. At last she began to speak.

"You told me that if I had something more to say about Mr Townsend you would be glad to listen to it."

"Exactly, my dear," said the Doctor, not turning around.

"I would like to see him again."

"To say goodbye?" asked the Doctor.

"No, father, not that. At least not forever."

"Have you written to him?"

"Yes, four times."

"You have not finished with him, then?"

"No," said Catherine. "I have asked him—asked him to wait."

The Doctor turned around slowly in his chair and looked at her with his cold eyes. She was afraid of his anger.

"You are a dear, faithful child," he said at last. "Come here to your father." And he got up, holding his hands towards her.

The words were a surprise and they gave her an exquisite joy. She went to him and he put his arm around her tenderly and kissed her. After this he said, "Do you wish to make me very happy?"

"I would like to, but I am afraid I can't," Catherine answered. "Do you want me to give him up?"

"Yes, I want you to give him up."

He continued holding her, looking into her face. She looked

---

1. **scratching** : noise a fountain pen makes when writing on paper.

away and there was a long silence.

"You are happier than I am, father," she said, at last.

"I have no doubt that you are unhappy now. But it is better to be unhappy for three months than for many years."

"Yes, if that were true," said Catherine.

"It is true, I am sure of that. Remember, I know something about men—their vices, [1] their selfishness, their falsities!" [2]

She moved away from him and said, "He is not vicious [3]—he is not false!"

"Don't you trust my judgment?" asked the Doctor.

"What has he done? What do you know?"

"He has never done anything—he is selfish and lazy."

"Oh, father, don't say bad things about him!" she exclaimed.

"No, that would be a great mistake. You may do what you choose," he added, turning away.

"I may see him again?"

"Just as you choose."

"Will you forgive me?"

"No!"

"I only want to see him once to tell him to wait."

"To wait for what?"

"To wait until you know him better—until you consent."

1. **vices** : evil or immoral actions.
2. **falsities** : lies.
3. **vicious** : cruel, dangerous.

"I know him well enough, and I will never consent."

"But we can wait a long time," said poor Catherine with humility.

"Of course, you can wait until I die, if you like."

Catherine gave a cry of natural horror.

"Your engagement will have one delightful effect upon you. It will make you extremely impatient for my death. And just think how impatient *he* will be too."

She turned away feeling sick. Suddenly, however, she had an inspiration.

"If I don't marry before your death, I will not after," she said."

"Do you want to be impertinent?" asked the Doctor.

"Impertinent? Oh, father, what terrible things you say!"

For some time Catherine was silent, but finally she said,

"I think that little by little Morris might persuade you."

"I shall never speak to him again. I dislike him too much."

Catherine gave a long sigh which she tried to cover. She had decided that it was wrong to make a show of her troubles and to influence her father with her emotions. Her desire was to bring about a gentle, gradual change in her father's opinion of Morris.

"There is one thing you can tell Mr Townsend when you see him again. Tell him that if you marry without my consent, I won't leave you a penny of my money. That will interest him more than anything else you can tell him."

"That would be very right," answered Catherine, "In that case I shouldn't receive any money from you."

She looked at her father and her quiet eyes were filled with tears.

"I think I will see him then," she murmured timidly.

"Exactly as you choose. But if you see him, you will be an ungrateful, cruel child. You will give your father the greatest pain of his life."

Tears ran down Catherine's face and she moved towards her parent with a pitiful cry. He simply took her arm, led her to the door and opened it for her. Then he closed the door gently but firmly behind her.

The Doctor walked around his study for a while, a bit irritated but also amused. He said to himself, "I believe she will go on with it!" This idea appeared to have a comical [1] side and to offer some entertainment.

---

1. **comical** : that makes you laugh.

Comprehension and personal response

1 **a.** What did Catherine do after her aunt had gone away?

b. What happened after her father had let her in?

c. Why did he think she only wanted to see Morris again to say goodbye?

  i. Catherine's placid behaviour had made him think she was ready to do exactly what he wanted.

  ii. He was very sure of himself so he took it for granted that his daughter would not resist him.

  iii. Deep down he despised his daughter as a young woman with a weak personality who would accept his judgment for lack of spirit.

d. Do you think it is possible that more than one of the explanations above (or all of them) are right?

e. Did Doctor Sloper accept Catherine's suggestion that he should try to get to know Morris better? What did he say?

f. Did Catherine submit to her father's will?

g. What was her mood when she left the room?

h. Was her father moved by her pain?

Words

2 Look at the following adjectives and choose those that in your opinion could apply to a father in Doctor Sloper's position:

> **disappointed   anxious   sad   glad   sympathetic**
> **pitiless   proud   puzzled   pained   irritated**
> **amused   angry   obstinate   strict   kind**

Now compare the adjectives of your choice to those used in the text to describe Doctor Sloper's feelings: is his reaction what you would have expected?

Listening

3 Listen to the CD from the beginning of the chapter to: "At last she began to speak" and fill in the gaps.

Catherine sat alone .... for more than an hour. Her aunt seemed to her .... She had an immense respect for her father and she felt that to displease him was ....; but her plan was slowly taking form and she had to .... When the clock struck eleven, and the house was in silence, Catherine slowly went to .... She knocked and her father opened the door.

"What is the matter?" asked the Doctor. "You are standing there like ....!"

She went into the room but it was some time before she began to speak. Her father ...., sat down and began writing. His back was turned to her and she heard the scratching .... At last she began to speak.

Grammar

4 Let's try to imagine what would have happened if...
To do that we need the so called "third conditional" which deals with things that could have happened in the past if certain conditions had occurred. Write sentences in the third conditional using the words in brackets.

a. If Catherine (*be*) beautiful, maybe Morris (*love*) her.

b. Her father (*be*) pleased, if Catherine (*leave*) Morris.

c. If Morris (*not be*) lazy, he (*not need*) a rich wife.

d. If Doctor Sloper (*understand*) how unhappy his daughter was, he (*not oppose*) her marriage.

e. Mrs Penniman (*advise*) Catherine better, if she (*not be*) foolish.

f. If Doctor Sloper (*like*) Morris, he (*give*) his consent to the marriage.

Catherine Chooses

The next day Doctor Sloper called Mrs Penniman into his library.

"I have called you here to advise you that I don't want you or Catherine to see Mr Townsend again. Anything you will do to help or comfort Catherine will be considered treason. [1] You know treason is a very serious offence." [2]

Mrs Penniman threw back her head and said, "Do you want to kill your child?"

"No, I want to make her live and be happy," replied the Doctor.

"You will kill her! She had a terrible night."

---

1. **treason** : crime of disloyalty or betrayal.
2. **offence** : insult.

"She won't die of one bad night, nor of a dozen. Remember that I am a distinguished physician."

Catherine had had a dreadful,[1] sleepless night. Her heart was breaking. She cried and thought about her father's harsh[2] words. She believed that she was bad, but she could not help it.

The next morning she did not want to show her pain to the world. Therefore, she came to breakfast on time, with no tears in her eyes, which disappointed Mrs Penniman. That day she wrote to Morris asking him to come and see her the next day.

Catherine received him in the big, bright front parlour. The first thing she noticed was that he was more beautiful than ever.

"Why have you made me wait so long?" he asked. "Every hour seemed like years. Have you decided whether you will keep me or give me up?"

"Oh, Morris," she cried, "I never thought of giving you up!"

"Then what were you waiting for?"

"I thought my father might—might look at it differently. But he still looks at it the same way."

---

1. **dreadful** : terrible, horrible.
2. **harsh** : hard, cruel.

"Then why have you called me here?"

"Because I wanted to see you," cried Catherine.

"Will you marry me tomorrow?" Morris suddenly asked.

"Tomorrow?"

"Next week, then—any time within a month?"

"Isn't it better to wait?" said Catherine.

"To wait for what?"

She did not know for what, but she was afraid. "Until we have thought about it a little more."

Morris shook his head sadly and said, "I thought *you* had thought about it in these three weeks. Do you want to think about it for the next five years? My poor girl, you are not sincere."

Catherine blushed and her eyes filled with tears. "Oh, how can you say that?" she murmured.

"You must take me or leave me," said Morris. "You can't please your father and me. You must choose between us."

"I have chosen you," she said passionately.

"Then marry me next week!"

She stood gazing at him. "Isn't there any other way?"

"None that I know of." He turned away, walked to the window and looked out. He finally said, "You are terribly afraid of your father."

"I suppose I must be," she said very simply.

"Then you don't love me as I love you. Your fear of your father seems greater than your love for me."

"Oh, my friend," said Catherine going to him.

"Do I fear anything?" he demanded, looking at her. "For you I would do anything!"

"You are noble and brave!"

Catherine knew that she had to deliver her father's message to Morris. It was very painful for her, but she said, "He told me to tell you very distinctly that if I marry without his consent, I shall not inherit a penny of his fortune. He made a great point of this. [1] He seemed to think—"

Morris blushed angrily and said, "What did he seem to think?"

"That it would make a difference."

"It *will* make a difference in many things. We will be poorer, but it will not change my love for you."

"We shall not want the money," said Catherine. "You know that I have my own fortune."

"Yes, my dear girl, I know you have something, and he can't touch that."

"He would never," said Catherine. "My mother left it to me."

Morris was silent for a while. "Do you think that he will be cruel to you forever? Do you think he will never change his mind about disinheriting you?"

"If I marry you he will think I am not good."

"Then he will never forgive you!" cried Morris.

The words disinherit and forgive, with their heavy moral meaning, rang in Catherine's ears, and deeply touched her childlike heart. She felt very lonely and afraid.

---

1. **made a great point of this** : considered it very important.

Catherine Chooses

"Oh, Morris," she cried, putting her head on his shoulder, "you must love me very much. I will marry you as soon as you want!"

"My dear good girl," he exclaimed, looking down at his prize. [1] Then he looked up again rather vaguely with parted lips and lifted eyebrows.

Life in Washington Square continued much as before for many days. Doctor Sloper told his sister Elizabeth that Catherine's situation amused him greatly, and that he was waiting with suspense to see the outcome.

Mrs Almond replied, "It is not very kind of you to find amusement in your daughter's situation."

"I want to take Catherine to Europe!" said the Doctor. "Europe will give Catherine new things to think about."

"She won't forget him in Europe," said Elizabeth.

"He will forget her then."

Mrs Almond looked serious. "Would you really like that?"

"Extremely," said the Doctor.

Meanwhile, Mrs Penniman, who was alarmed [2] by her brother's coldness towards her, arranged another secret meeting with Morris Townsend. This time she did not choose an oyster saloon. She asked him to meet her at the door of a church.

"I come as a messenger of peace," said Mrs Penniman. "I

---

1. **prize** : something of value that is gained after a struggle.
2. **alarmed** : frightened or worried.

think you should wait a while before marrying Catherine."

Morris Townsend was quite annoyed. "You have many different ways of seeing the same problem. Last week you advised me to marry her immediately!"

"Be very patient, watch and wait! Wait until my brother is less angry," said Mrs Penniman.

"Catherine has already agreed to marry me very soon," said Morris. "What can I do now?"

"Catherine loves you so much that you can do anything you want," said Mrs Penniman. "You can change your plans and she won't get upset."

Morris looked at her with raised eyebrows and simply said "Ah!" After he had accompanied her home he considered his dilemma. [1] It was not easy for him to choose between the fear of losing Catherine and her possible fortune altogether, and the fear of taking her too soon and being tied to a young woman who was both unattractive and impoverished. [2]

---

1. **dilemma** : a situation in which you have to make a difficult choice between two or more things.
2. **impoverished** : very poor.

Comprehension

1 **Put the following sentences in the correct sequence without looking back at the text.**

a. Morris offered to marry Catherine immediately but she suggested they should wait.

b. Doctor Sloper told his sister Lavinia that he would consider her a traitor if she helped Catherine or saw Morris.

c. Morris didn't want to be married to a woman who was plain and no longer very rich.

d. Mrs Penniman advised Morris to wait before he married Catherine.

e. Catherine said she would marry Morris as soon as he wanted.

f. Catherine had to tell Morris that her father would disinherit her if she married without his consent.

g. Catherine was suffering terribly but she didn't want to show her pain.

h. Doctor Sloper told his sister Elizabeth he would take Catherine to Europe.

i. Catherine asked Morris to come and see her.

Words

2 **Match the following definitions with the right words from the text.**

a. take an object / a letter / a parcel / a message to a place or a person it is addressed to (*verb*): ....

b. become red in the face because of shame or embarrassment (*verb*): ....

c. the crime of being disloyal to your country, generally by helping its enemies; betrayal of trust (*noun*): ....

d. successful and therefore respected and admired (*adjective*):
....

e. the line of hair above the eyes (*noun*): ....

f. pardon or show mercy to somebody (*verb*): ....

g. the feeling that you have when you think that something is funny (*noun*): ....

h. illegal act, crime (*noun*): ....

Listening

 3 Fill in the blanks using the words listed below, then check your answers listening to the CD from: "Meanwhile, Mrs Penniman..." to "...and simply said 'Ah!'"

> **less   upset   door   agreed   coldness**
> **messenger   annoyed   raised   advised   secret**

Meanwhile, Mrs Penniman, who was alarmed by her brother's
¹ .... towards her, arranged another ² .... meeting
with Morris Townsend. This time she did not choose an oyster
saloon. She asked him to meet her at the ³ .... of a church.

"I come as a ⁴ .... of peace," said Mrs Penniman. "I think
you should wait a while before marrying Catherine."

Morris Townsend was quite ⁵ .... "You have many
different ways of seeing the same problem. Last week you
⁶ .... me to marry her immediately!"

"Be very patient, watch and wait! Wait until my brother is
⁷ .... angry," said Mrs Penniman.

"Catherine has already ⁸ .... to marry me very soon," said
Morris. "What can I do now?"

"Catherine loves you so much that you can do anything you want," said Mrs Penniman. "You can change your plans and she won't get **9** ...."

Morris looked at her with **10** .... eyebrows and simply said, "Ah!"

Language Production

4 Imagine Morris is writing a letter to a friend in Europe explaining his situation. You can begin like this:

Dear Rudolf,

You know what a confirmed bachelor I used to be, and yet I might marry sooner than my friends think! I have spent most of my fortune but I like my comforts and I don't intend to give them up, so a rich heiress is going to pay for them. Of course she's no beauty (one can't have everything!) and to tell the truth she's also deadly boring but she loves me and will never give me up. Unfortunately, there is a serious problem. Her father

....

....

CHAPTER 15

Europe

Mrs Penniman did not mention her meeting with Morris Townsend to Catherine, who was very quiet. She had not spoken to her father since the evening in his study. The Doctor was cold and absolutely [1] indifferent to the presence of his daughter and his sister.

However, Catherine had something to say to her father. "I think we shall marry—before very long. And I shall probably see him about once a week—not more."

The Doctor looked at her coldly from head to foot. "Why do you tell me this? It doesn't matter to me."

There were tears in Catherine's eyes as she cried, "Oh, father, don't you care?"

"Not at all. Once you marry it is the same to me when, where

---

1. **absolutely** : completely.

or why you do it."

The next day he spoke to her in a different manner. "Are you going to marry in the next four or five months?" the Doctor asked.

"I don't know, father," answered Catherine. "It is not easy for us to decide."

"Wait then, for six months, and I will take you to Europe. I would very much like you to go."

After the words of the day before, Catherine was delighted to hear that her father was still interested in her. "It would be delightful to go to Europe!" she said. But her happiness soon faded [1] when she realized that she would not see Morris for months.

"Very well, we will go. Go and pack your clothes."

Mrs Penniman was obviously not invited, and she understood why the Doctor had made this plan. She told Catherine, "He thinks the trip to Europe will make you forget Morris."

Since Catherine was going to Europe to please her father, she suddenly felt freer and more determined. Now, at last, her passion possessed her completely.

She wrote to Morris asking him to meet her in the Square the next day. They took a long walk and she told him about her father's invitation to visit Europe. Morris asked her many questions as they walked. One particular question struck her: "Would you like to see all those beautiful things over there?"

"Oh no, Morris!" said Catherine.

"Goodness, what a dull woman!" Morris thought to himself.

"He thinks I will forget you," said Catherine.

---

1. **faded** : disappeared.

"Well, my dear, perhaps you will."

"Please don't say that," Catherine answered gently.

"You should go," Morris said. "It will please your father and perhaps he will forgive you and change his mind about disinheriting you."

"And not get married for so long?"

"We can marry when you return, and you can buy your wedding clothes in Paris."

Europe

Doctor Sloper and his daughter visited Europe for twelve months, and not six. During the first six months of their trip the Doctor never spoke to Catherine about their difference. There were so many things in Europe that interested him. Catherine was quiet, docile, punctual and obedient. She neither appreciated nor criticised what she saw and her father judged her a very unintelligent travelling companion.

One day at the end of the summer the two travellers were walking together in a lonely valley of the Alps. It was late in the afternoon and the air was getting cold. Catherine felt lonely in this desolate place. The Doctor suddenly looked at her and asked, "Have you given him up?"

The question was unexpected, but Catherine did not hesitate. "No, father," she answered.

He looked at her without speaking.

"Does he write to you?"

"Yes, about twice a month."

The Doctor looked at the valley and said in a low voice, "I am very angry. You try [1] my patience. I am not a very good man and I can be very hard."

"I am sorry," Catherine murmured. Her heart grew cold and she felt frightened.

"One day he will leave you, alone and hungry, in a desolate place like this."

"That is not true, father!"

He did not speak to her about Morris for another six months.

---

1. **try** : test.

Washington Square

The night before sailing to New York the Doctor asked her, "What are you going to do when you get home?"

"Do you mean about Mr Townsend?"

"About Mr Townsend."

"We shall probably marry."

"So you will go off with him as soon as you arrive?"

This seemed like a vulgar [1] way of putting it and Catherine resented [2] it. "I cannot tell you until we arrive," she said.

"All I ask of you is that you *do* tell me. When a poor man is going to lose his child, he would like to know before it happens."

"Oh, father, you will not lose me," Catherine cried.

When Catherine arrived in New York she did not "go off" with Morris Townsend. Morris was, of course, the natural subject of conversation between Catherine and her aunt.

"I have seen a lot of Morris while you were away. I think I know him well; he is full of passion and energy," said Mrs Penniman. Catherine listened with interest and apprehension [3] as her aunt told her that Morris used to sit in the Doctor's study, smoke his cigars and look at his books.

While Catherine and her father were in Europe, Mrs Almond had told her sister that she was behaving foolishly. "You should not be so friendly with him. If he marries her and she doesn't get Austin's money, he will hate Catherine and be cruel to her."

Catherine listened to Mrs Penniman and said, "I wish he had found some employment."

---

1. **vulgar** : rude.
2. **resented** : felt angry about something.
3. **apprehension** : worry or fear about something in the future.

"He has found some employment. He told me to tell you as soon as you arrived. He has formed a partnership with a commission merchant." [1]

"Oh, I'm so glad!" exclaimed Catherine.

"How is your father? Is he still implacable?" [2] Mrs Penniman asked.

"Oh, yes. Europe has made him more determined, more terrible. I shall never change him and I expect nothing from him now," answered Catherine.

"I didn't think you would give up your property," said Mrs Penniman. "You have become very brave."

"Yes, I am braver than I was. You asked me if I had changed; I have changed in that way. I have changed very much. If Morris doesn't care about it, why should I?" said Catherine.

"Perhaps he *does* care about it," insisted Mrs Penniman.

"He cares about it for me, because he doesn't want to injure me. But Morris knows that I am not afraid of that. Besides, I have plenty of money of my own. We shall live well," Catherine replied.

Catherine had indeed changed. Mrs Penniman found her improved in appearance; she looked rather handsome. Her tone was sharper, more authoritative. [3] Her feelings about her father had changed. She had been as good as she could, but he did not care. And now, for the first time, she did not care either. She had come home to get married.

---

1. **commission merchant** : trade agent.
2. **implacable** : that cannot be changed.
3. **authoritative** : showing authority.

BLACK CAT ENGLISH CLUB

The Commercial Press (Hong Kong) Ltd.
9/F, Eastern Central Plaza,
3 Yiu Hing Road, Shau Kei Wan,
Hong Kong

BLACK CAT ENGLISH CLUB
Membership Application Form

BLACK CAT ENGLISH CLUB is for those who love English reading and seek for better English to share and learn with fun together.

Benefits offered: - *Member Card*

  - *Member badge, poster, bookmark*

  - *Book discount coupon*

  - *Black Cat English Reward Scheme*

  - *English learning e-forum*

  - *Surprise gift and more...*

Simply fill out the application form below and fax it back to 2565 1113.

Join Now! It's FREE exclusively for readers who have purchased *Black Cat English Readers* !

The book(or book set) that you have purchased: _____

English Name: _____ (Surname) _____ (Given Name)

Chinese Name: _____

Address: _____

Tel: _____ Fax: _____

Email: _____

Sex: ❏ Male ❏ Female (Login password for e-forum will be sent to this email address.)

Education Background: ❏ Primary 1-3 ❏ Primary 4-6 ❏ Junior Secondary Education (F1-3)

  ❏ Senior Secondary Education (F4-5) ❏ Matriculation

  ❏ College ❏ University or above

Age: ❏ 6 - 9 ❏ 10 - 12 ❏ 13 - 15 ❏ 16 - 18 ❏ 19 - 24 ❏ 25 - 34

  ❏ 35 - 44 ❏ 45 - 54 ❏ 55 or above

Occupation: ❏ Student ❏ Teacher ❏ White Collar ❏ Blue Collar

  ❏ Professional ❏ Manager ❏ Business Owner ❏ Housewife

  ❏ Others (please specify: _____)

As a member, what would you like **BLACK CAT ENGLISH CLUB** to offer:

  ❏ Member gathering/ party ❏ English class with native teacher ❏ English competition

  ❏ Newsletter ❏ Online sharing ❏ Book fair

  ❏ Book discount ❏ Others (please specify: _____)

Other suggestions to **BLACK CAT ENGLISH CLUB**:

_____

Please sign here: _____

(Date: _____)

Comprehension and personal response

1 **a.** Was Doctor Sloper as indifferent to his daughter's decision as he pretended to be?

b. Was Catherine pleased that her father wanted to take her to Europe? Why?

c. Why do you think Mrs Penniman wasn't invited?

d. Why wasn't Catherine interested in what she was going to see in Europe? Do you think it was because she was dull?

e. What did Morris advise her to do?

f. How long did the Slopers stay in Europe?

g. When and where did father and daughter eventually discuss Catherine's situation?

h. What did the Doctor ask Catherine the night before leaving Europe?

i. What had Mrs Penniman done in the meantime? Had her sister approved of her behaviour? Why? / Why not?

j. Was Catherine still concerned about her father's disapproval?

Character

2 Scan the text and make a list of all the adjectives used to describe Catherine in this chapter. Are there any changes from the way she has been described so far?

Listening

3 Listen to the CD from: "When Catherine arrived in New York..." to: "...a commission merchant", then see if you can remember enough to fill the gaps without listening again.

When Catherine arrived in New York she did not .... with Morris Townsend . Morris was, of course, the natural subject of conversation between Catherine and ....

"I have seen a lot of Morris while you were away. I think I know him well; he is full of ....," said Mrs Penniman. Catherine listened with interest and apprehension as her aunt told her that Morris .... in the Doctor's study, smoke his cigars and look at his books.

While Catherine and her father ...., Mrs Almond had told her sister that she was behaving foolishly. "You should not .... with him. If he marries her and she doesn't get Austin's money, he will hate Catherine and be cruel ...."

Catherine listened to Mrs Penniman and said, "I wish he had found some employment."

"He has .... He told me to tell you as soon as you arrived. He has formed .... with a commission merchant."

If you haven't filled in all the gaps, listen to your CD and try again!

Grammar

4 "I wish he had found some employment" Catherine told Mrs Penniman while they were talking about Morris. You use *wish* with the Past Perfect to express regret for something that happened (or didn't happen) in the past.
Make sentences using *wish* with the Past Perfect.

a. Catherine – wish – Morris – find employment.

b. Catherine – wish – her father – be more gentle to her.

c. Mrs Penniman – wish – her brother – change his mind.

d. Morris – wish – Catherine – be interested in Europe.

e. Mrs Penniman – wish – Morris – not care about money.

f. Doctor Sloper – wish – Catherine – not write to Morris.

CHAPTER 16

Morris's Decision

The next day in the afternoon Morris Townsend came to visit Catherine, who received him in the front parlour.

"I am very glad you have come back," he said. "It makes me very happy to see you again." And he looked at her, smiling, from head to toe, although it didn't appear afterward that he found her more attractive.

To Catherine he appeared splendid. She could hardly believe that this beautiful young man was her own property. Catherine asked him about his new business and Morris asked her about Europe. Without waiting for him to ask, she told him about her father.

"We must not expect his money now," she said, "and we must live without it."

Morris smiled and said, "My poor, dear girl!"

"You mustn't pity [1] me," said Catherine. "I don't mind it now."

Morris got up and walked around the room. "Let me talk to him. I am much wiser now, I have more tact."

"Please don't, Morris; please don't," she said with a certain sad firmness [2] in her voice, which he heard for the first time. "We must ask him no favours. [3] I know that he will never change."

"Why not?"

"He is not very fond of me," she said hesitantly. "It is because he was so fond of my mother, whom we lost long ago. She was beautiful and very, very clever. He is always thinking of her. I am not at all like her. My Aunt Lavinia told me so. Of course, it isn't my fault, but it isn't his fault either. I think he despises [4] me. The night before we sailed for New York he spoke to me in such a way that I will never forget. That night I firmly decided that I would never ask him for anything again, or expect anything from him."

"What a strange family!" said Morris.

"Don't say that—don't say anything unkind. You must be very kind to me now, because—because I have done a great deal for you."

"Oh, I know that, my dear."

---

1. **pity** : feel sorry for.
2. **firmness** : determination.
3. **favours** : kind treatment.
4. **despises** : considers worthless or inferior.

Morris's Decision

"It has been terrible for me to be separated from my father, to feel that he despises me. I would be extremely unhappy if I didn't love you. We must be very happy together. And Morris, you must never despise me!" Catherine's voice was full of emotion as she spoke.

This was an easy promise to make and Morris made it. But he made no other promises.

After his return Doctor Sloper had many things to discuss with his sisters. "I imagine you saw Mr Townsend very frequently during Catherine's absence, and consoled [1] him," he said to Lavinia. "Don't tell me. I don't want to know. There is something in this house that tells me that Mr Townsend has sat in these chairs and warmed himself by that fire. I don't know what you have told him, but my opinion of him remains the same."

He told his sister Elizabeth that he was no longer amused by Catherine; he was quite irritated and exasperated. [2]

"She will never give Mr Townsend up," said Mrs Almond.

"Then she will be very unhappy and I can't prevent it," said the Doctor.

Mrs Penniman immediately wrote to Morris Townsend and arranged another secret meeting. She felt like Morris's mother or sister, and had a great desire to make him comfortable and happy.

---

1. **consoled** : comforted.
2. **exasperated** : made angry.

During a long walk Mrs Penniman told Morris in detail what the Doctor had said.

"He will never give us a penny," said Morris angrily. "A man should know when he has lost," he added. "I must give her up!"

Mrs Penniman received this declaration in silence, but it made her heart beat a little. "I think I understand you," she said gently. "My poor Morris, do you know how much she loves you?"

Morris was ashamed of himself. He felt vicious and cruel. "No, I don't. I don't want to know. It would be too painful."

"Catherine will suffer greatly."

"You must console her. The Doctor will help you. He will be delighted that the engagement is broken. He will invent something to comfort her."

"He will say, 'I always told you so!' "

Morris blushed bright red. "This is all very unpleasant. A true friend would try to make it easy for me."

"Would you like me to tell her?" Mrs Penniman asked.

"You mustn't tell her, but you can explain that I don't want to come between her and her father."

"Will you come to see her again?"

"Oh, I shall come again, but I have been to see her four times since she came back, and it is very hard work."

"Ah, but you must have your last parting!" [1] Mrs Penniman exclaimed, whose idea of the last parting was almost as romantic as the first meeting.

---

1. **parting** : leaving.

Comprehension and personal response

1 **Read the following statements and decide whether they are true (T) or false (F). Then correct the false ones.**

		T	F
a.	Morris thought Catherine looked more attractive than before.	☐	☐
b.	When Morris asked her, Catherine told him about her father	☐	☐
c.	Catherine firmly refused to ask any favours of her father.	☐	☐
d.	Doctor Sloper had not been very fond of Catherine's mother.	☐	☐
e.	Catherine had suffered a lot when she had realized that her father despised her.	☐	☐
f.	Doctor Sloper realized that Lavinia had often invited Morris to the house during his absence.	☐	☐
g.	Mrs Almond said Catherine would be very unhappy if she married Mr Townsend.	☐	☐
h.	Morris told Mrs Penniman he had to leave Catherine.	☐	☐
i.	Morris didn't care about Catherine's misery.	☐	☐
j.	Mrs Penniman told Morris he shouldn't give Catherine the pain of the last parting.	☐	☐

Character

2 **Answer the following questions.**

a. How has Catherine's personality changed after her trip to Europe? What do you think has changed her?

b. Consider Morris Townsend's behaviour: why is he preparing to break off his engagement to Catherine? Read the following explanations and choose the one that seems right to you:

    i. He used to be in love with Catherine but she has been away too long and he has stopped loving her.

    ii. He has been after [1] the money all the time and now he doesn't want to marry a girl who is less rich than he expected her to be.

    iii. He doesn't want Catherine to break off relations with her father and become impoverished.

Words

3 You have already met a certain number of words relating to physical appearance. In this chapter for example you have found: *attractive, splendid, beautiful.* Add more words to the spidergram below. A few have already been added for you.

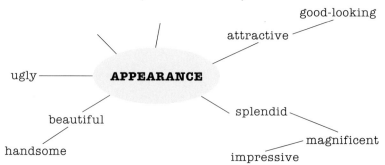

If you can't remember many more words, look for synonyms in your monolingual dictionary.

---

1. **after** : looking for.

Grammar

4 "He was so fond of my mother, whom we lost long ago." You have already met a number of relative clauses, both in this chapter and the previous ones. Complete the following sentences using *who, whom, whose* and *which* where necessary.

a. Catherine Sloper was a young woman .... lived in New York.

b. She fell in love with a young man .... family was not very rich.

c. The man .... she loved was called Morris Townsend.

d. Morris had a sister with .... he lived.

e. They lived on Second Avenue in a house .... was very small.

f. Catherine's father was a doctor .... ability was highly respected.

g. Doctor Sloper had two sisters: Lavinia .... he didn't like very much and Elizabeth .... was his favourite.

Meanings

5 Look back at the text and write down:

a. the sentence that means Morris didn't notice the improvement in Catherine's looks;
....

b. the sentences that describe the feelings Doctor Sloper had had for his wife;
....

c. the sentences that show Morris can feel some shame about his own actions;
....

d. the sentence that shows how unpleasant it is for Morris to visit Catherine now.
....

CHAPTER 17

The Parting

He came again and again without managing the last parting. It was awkward [1] for him and he had developed a strong dislike for Catherine's aunt, who, as he said, had put him into this mess. [2] Catherine suspected nothing. She looked at her lover with eyes of complete trust. Mrs Penniman wandered about the house very uncomfortably with her unexploded bomb in her hands.

Catherine waited patiently for Morris to name the day of their wedding. His visits were very brief and he had very little to talk about. Catherine began to worry.

"Are you sick?" she asked Morris. "You seem so restless." [3]

---

1. **awkward** : difficult, embarrassing, unpleasant.
2. **mess** : trouble, difficult situation.
3. **restless** : never calm, always moving about.

The Parting

"I am not at all well," said Morris. "I have to go away."

"Go away? Where are you going, Morris?"

He looked at her and for a moment she was afraid of him. "Will you promise not to make a scene?" [1]

"A scene? Do I make scenes?" asked Catherine.

"I have to go away on business—to New Orleans."

"Take me with you!"

"Take you with me—on business?"

"What is your business? Your business is to be with me."

Morris told her a long story about an opportunity he had to make six thousand dollars buying cotton.

Catherine took his arm in her two hands and spoke with more force than he had ever heard before.

"You can go to New Orleans another time. This isn't the moment; we have waited too long already."

"Very well, then, we won't talk about it any more. I will do my business by letter."

"You won't go?"

Morris wanted to provoke [2] a quarrel, it was the easiest way to break away from her.

"You are not discreet. You must not tell me what to do," he said. "Try and be calmer the next time I come."

"When will you come again?"

"I will come next Saturday," said Morris.

---

1. **make a scene** : express great anger, lose your temper.
2. **provoke** : cause.

"Come tomorrow," Catherine begged, "I want you to come tomorrow. I will be very quiet." She suddenly felt frightened and wanted to keep him in the room.

Morris kissed her forehead and Catherine's heart beat very fast. "Will you promise to come tomorrow?" she asked gently.

"I said Saturday!" Morris answered smiling. He tried to be angry at one moment and smile at the next. Everything seemed so awkward and unpleasant.

"Yes, Saturday too," she answered trying to smile. "But tomorrow first." He was going to the door and she went with him quickly. She would do anything to keep him.

"I am a busy man!" cried Morris sternly. His voice was so hard and unnatural that she turned away with a helpless look. He quickly put his hand on the doorknob. [1] In a moment she was close to him again. "Morris, you are going to leave me."

"Yes, for a little while. Until you are reasonable again."

"I shall never be reasonable, in that way." And she tried to keep him longer. "Think of what I have done!" she cried. "Morris, I have given up everything."

"You shall have everything back."

"You wouldn't say that if you didn't mean something. What is it? What has happened? What have I done? What has changed you?"

"I will write to you—that is better."

"Ah, you won't come back!" she cried, bursting into tears.

---

1. **doorknob** : round knob turned to open a door.

The Parting

"Dear Catherine," he said, "don't believe that. I promise you that you shall see me again." He managed to get away and close the door behind him.

It was almost the last outbreak of passion of her life, but it was long and terrible. She threw herself on the sofa, buried her head in the cushions and cried desperately. It seemed to her that a mask had suddenly fallen from his face. He had wanted to get away from her. He had been angry and cruel.

Catherine wanted to believe that he would return. She listened, hoping to hear his ring at the door. But Morris did not return, nor did he call or write the next day. Catherine wrote him two notes, one on Friday and one on Saturday. "I don't understand," she wrote. "Morris, you are killing me!"

Catherine suffered deeply, but she did not want her father to know what had happened. She ate her meals, went on with her life and said nothing to anyone.

Mrs Penniman felt that something was wrong. She approached Catherine very gently and said, "I am afraid you are in trouble, my dear. Can I do anything to help you?"

"I am not in any trouble and do not need any help," said Catherine.

"Are you very sure, dear?"

"Perfectly sure."

Some days passed and the Doctor, who had been observing everything in silence, spoke to his sister Lavinia.

Washington Square

"The thing has happened—the scoundrel [1] has left her!"

"It seems to make you happy to see your daughter upset!"

"It does," said the Doctor, "because it proves I was right."

On Sunday afternoon Catherine went for a walk and found Mrs Penniman waiting for her when she returned.

"Where have you been?" asked Mrs Penniman.

"I went to take a walk," answered Catherine.

"Catherine dear, you cannot pretend with me. I know everything, and I really think it is better that you separate."

"Separate. Who said we were going to separate?"

"Isn't it broken off?" asked Mrs Penniman.

"My engagement? Not at all!"

"In that case I have spoken too soon. I am sorry. But something has certainly happened between you," insisted Mrs Penniman.

"Nothing has happened. I love him more and more!"

Mrs Penniman was silent for an instant. "I suppose that's why you went to see him this afternoon."

Catherine blushed. "Yes, I went to see him! But that's my own business."

"Very well, then, we won't talk about it." Mrs Penniman moved towards the door, but was stopped by a sudden cry from the girl.

"Aunt Lavinia, *where* has he gone? At his house they said he had left town. Has he gone to New Orleans?"

Mrs Penniman did not know about New Orleans. She only

---

1. **scoundrel** : wicked, selfish man.

said, "If you have agreed to separate, the further he goes, the better."

"Agreed? Has he agreed it with you?"

"He has sometimes asked for my advice."

"Is it you, then, that has changed him? Is it you that has taken him from me? How could you be so cruel? You spoil everything you touch! Leave me alone!" Catherine spoke bitterly and vehemently. [1]

"You are a most ungrateful girl!" cried Mrs Penniman. "I helped bring you together."

"I wish he had never come to this house!" She calmed herself with great effort, and then got up and walked around the room.

"Will you please tell me where he is?"

"I have no idea," said Mrs Penniman.

"Will he stay away forever?"

"Forever is a long time. Your father, perhaps, won't live forever."

Catherine gazed at her aunt. "He has planned it then. He has broken it off, and given me up."

"For the present, dear Catherine. He has only put it off." [2]

"He has left me alone," Catherine said, shaking her head. "I don't believe it!"

---

1. **vehemently** : with strong feeling.
2. **put it off** : moved something to a later time.

Comprehension and personal response

1 **Put the following sentences in the correct sequence without looking back at the text.**

a. He said he was only going to leave her for a little while but he would write to her.

b. Mrs Penniman told Catherine she had better accept the separation and Catherine understood that Morris had left her.

c. Catherine wanted him to stay and told him he could go to New Orleans another time.

d. He said he wouldn't be back before the following Saturday because he was a busy man.

e. Morris wanted to find a way to break the engagement, so he told Catherine he had to go to New Orleans on business.

f. Catherine had a terrible time but she didn't show her father she was suffering.

g. Morris said she must not tell him what to do.

h. Catherine told Morris he was trying to leave her.

Character

2 **a. What do you think was Mrs Penniman's attitude during this crisis? Choose one of the suggestions below.**

i. She tried not to see the truth and was ready to protect Morris, thinking that his reasons were noble and unselfish.

ii. She realized Morris had never been in love with Catherine and she felt terribly sorry for her.

iii. She was embarrassed by the part she had had in the whole business and blamed Catherine for what had happened.

b. Why was it difficult for Morris to find a way to break with Catherine?

    i.   Because he did have some affection for her and didn't want her to suffer.

    ii.   Because he still hoped Catherine would inherit her father's money.

    iii. Because he didn't like to face anything unpleasant.

Writing

3 **"On Sunday afternoon Catherine went for a walk..."**
Where had Catherine really been? Imagine she is writing in her diary for that day. Write a few lines giving an account of her "walk". You can start like this:

I was so desperate that I could no longer stay at home waiting for him so I decided to go ...

Words

4 **Scan the text and find the phrasal verbs that mean:**

    a.   suddenly escape (generally from captivity)

    b.   part with something; renounce something

    c.   leave

    d.   stay where one is until somebody arrives or something happens

    e.   end something suddenly

    f.   postpone something

Grammar

5 Complete the following sentences using the phrasal verbs you have found in the exercise on the previous page.

a. Why are you so late? I've been .... you for almost one hour.

b. He has .... smoking.

c. Why do you keep .... the meeting ....?

d. The diplomatic relations between the two countries were
....

e. I want to .... from all this and have a real holiday.

f. The prisoner managed to .... from his guards.

Listening

 6 The following sentences, taken from the first paragraph, are in scrambled order. Try to put them in their correct order and then listen to the CD and check your answers.

a. She looked at her lover with eyes of complete trust.

b. It was awkward for him and he had developed a strong dislike for Catherine's aunt, who, as he said, had put him into this mess.

c. He came again and again without managing the last parting.

d. Mrs Penniman wandered about the house very uncomfortably with her unexploded bomb in her hands.

e. Catherine suspected nothing.

CHAPTER 18

The Letter

On Tuesday Catherine finally received a five-page letter from Morris. The letter was written in Philadelphia and it explained that he would be away on business for a long time. He said that he did not want to come between her and her fortune, and that he would never forget her. He wanted her to have a peaceful and happy life, and he hoped that one day they would meet as friends.

The letter caused poor Catherine an immense and long-lasting pain. She was too proud to say anything about it to her father or her aunt.

Her father waited a week before walking into the back parlour and saying, "I would like to know when you plan to leave this house."

Catherine looked up at him with a long, silent gaze and said, "I shall not go away!"

The Doctor raised his eyebrows and asked, "Has he left you?"

"I have broken off the engagement."

"Broken it off?"

"I have asked him to leave New York, and he has gone away for a long time."

The Doctor was both puzzled and disappointed. He lost his chance to say that he had been right. However, he did not believe what Catherine had said.

"How does he like your dismissal?" [1]

"I don't know!" said Catherine.

"You mean you don't care? You are rather cruel, after encouraging him and playing with him for so long!"

The Doctor had his revenge, after all.

As time went on the truth about the end of Catherine's engagement remained a closely guarded secret. She had suffered tremendously, [2] but the Doctor did not know about it. He was certainly curious to learn the truth, but he never knew it. This was his punishment for having been so very sarcastic [3] with his daughter.

"I am very glad that Catherine did not marry him," Mrs Almond said to her brother. "However, I wish you would be more gentle with her. Surely you feel sorry for her?"

"No, I don't. She was lucky to get out of it. Actually, I

---

1. **dismissal** : sending someone away.
2. **tremendously** : very much.
3. **sarcastic** : making somebody look silly.

suspect that she has not given him up at all. I think there is an arrangement between them. When I am dead, he will return and then they will marry."

"You accuse your daughter of being the worst of hypocrites," [1] said Mrs Almond.

 The years passed and Catherine received two offers of marriage. She refused a widower with three little girls and a clever young lawyer who was seriously in love with her. The name Morris Townsend was never mentioned at Washington Square, but Doctor Sloper still suspected that Catherine was secretly waiting for him.

Catherine had become an admirable old maid. [2] She formed habits and dedicated many of her days to charitable institutions. The two great facts of her life were that Morris Townsend had played with her heart and that her feelings towards her father would never be what they had been when she was younger. There was something dead in her life and her duty was to fill the void. [3] She had at last become a greatly liked figure at all respectable parties and dinners.

Doctor Sloper slowly retired from his profession. He went to Europe again with Catherine and Mrs Penniman, and remained there two years.

---

1. **hypocrites** : people who pretend to have feelings and opinions that they do not really have.
2. **old maid** : woman who never marries.
3. **void** : empty space.

Washington Square

One day, after his return from Europe, the Doctor said something to his daughter that surprised her greatly.

"I would like you to promise me something before I die."

"Why do you talk about your death?" she asked.

"Because I am sixty-eight years old, and one day I shall die. Promise me not to marry Morris Townsend after I am gone."

For a few minutes she said nothing, "Why do you speak of him?" she asked at last.

"He has been to New York recently and at your cousin Marian's house. Your Aunt Elizabeth tells me that he is looking for another wife, although I don't know what happened to the first one. He has grown fat and bald and has not made his fortune."

The words "fat" and "bald" presented a strange image to Catherine, who still remembered him as the most beautiful young man in the world. "I don't think you understand," she said. "I very rarely think of Mr Townsend. But I can't promise that."

The Doctor was silent for a minute. "I ask you for a particular reason. I am changing my will."

Catherine had been so humble in her youth, but now she had a little pride, and there was something in her father's request that injured her dignity.

"I can't promise," she simply repeated.

"You are very obstinate. [1] I had no idea how obstinate you are!"

She knew that she was obstinate, and it gave her a certain joy. She was now a middle-aged woman.

---

1. **obstinate** : refusing to change one's opinion.

Comprehension and personal response

1 **Read the following statements and decide whether they are true (T) or false (F). Then correct the false ones.**

		T	F
a.	Morris sent Catherine a short letter from New Orleans.	☐	☐
b.	Catherine's pain was terrible.	☐	☐
c.	Catherine told her father it was she who had broken off the engagement.	☐	☐
d.	Doctor Sloper knew the truth about the end of Catherine's engagement.	☐	☐
e.	Catherine never received an offer of marriage again.	☐	☐
f.	She was secretly waiting for Morris.	☐	☐
g.	Catherine had become an old maid.	☐	☐
h.	Doctor Sloper told Catherine she could marry Morris after his death.	☐	☐
i.	Morris was back in New York but he had changed a lot physically.	☐	☐
j.	Doctor Sloper told Catherine he was changing his will.	☐	☐

Character

2 **Answer the following questions.**

a. There is one person in Catherine's life whose opinions are generally kind and sensible. Who is this person?

b. We know Doctor Sloper was right from the start and yet we do not always approve of his behaviour as a father. Think back and try to list both the things you like in his behaviour and those you dislike.

Good Points: ....

Bad Points: ....

c. Two important facts have changed Catherine and both of them are very painful to her. One is Morris's deception. What do you think is the other one?

Language production

3 **a.** The first paragraph of this chapter tells us the content of Morris's letter to Catherine. Try to rewrite the letter (but make it much shorter than the original one!).

b. Try to give a description of the person Catherine has become. Before you do that, scan the text and find the two words related to Catherine that you have not found in previous descriptions of her personality:

P _ _ _ _

O _ _ _ _ _ _ _

Listening

4 Listen to the CD from: "The years passed..." to: "...parties and dinners". After you have listened, try to remember the right word and underline it. Then listen again and check your answers.

The years passed and Catherine received two (1 *proposals / offers / propositions*) of marriage. She refused a (2 *widower / gentleman / bachelor*) with three little girls and a (3 *brilliant / clever / successful*) young lawyer who was seriously in love with her. The name Morris Townsend was never mentioned at Washington Square, but Doctor Sloper still (4 *suspected / thought / imagined*) that Catherine was secretly waiting for him.

Catherine had become an admirable old (⁵ *woman / spinster / maid*).
She formed habits and dedicated many of her days to charitable
institutions. The two great facts of her life were that Morris
Townsend had (⁶ *played / trifled / tampered*) with her heart and that
her feelings towards her father would never be what they had been
when she was younger. There was something (⁷ *missing / finished /
dead*) in her life and her duty was to fill the void. She had at last
become a greatly liked figure at all (⁸ *elegant / respectable / formal*)
parties and dinners.

Grammar

5 "He lost his chance to say he had been right. *However*, he did not
believe..."

**Use linkers to fill the gaps in the following sentences. Sometimes
you may be able to think of more than one.**

a. .... Catherine had refused all marriage proposals, her
father still thought she had an agreement with Morris Townsend.

b. Catherine was suffering terribly. .... , she was
determined not to show it.

c. Doctor Sloper was pleased the engagement had been broken off,
.... he was still very suspicious.

d. .... Catherine received Morris's letter, she was
heartbroken.

e. Morris had never cared for Catherine .... she had
loved him with all her heart.

CHAPTER 19

The Will

A nother year passed and Doctor Sloper became very ill. After a three-week illness, during which Catherine and Mrs Penniman were always at his bedside, he died.

When his will was opened it was discovered that he had changed it shortly before his death. Catherine received only a fifth of his property. "She is well provided for from her mother's side," the will read. "Her fortune is already more than sufficient to attract those unscrupulous [1] adventurers whom she regards as an interesting class." He left the rest of his fortune to several different hospitals and schools of medicine in various cities. Mrs Penniman thought that the will was cruel and unjust, but Catherine simply said, "I like it very much. I only wish it had been expressed differently."

---

1. **unscrupulous** : without moral principles.

The Will

Catherine and her aunt continued to live in the big house in Washington Square. Catherine usually spent the month of August at a hotel at the seaside.

One warm summer evening in July the two ladies were sitting in front of an open window and Mrs Penniman said, "Catherine, I have something to say that will surprise you." She paused and then said, "I have seen Morris Townsend."

Catherine remained still. Then she said, "I hope he was well."

"I don't know. He is changed. He would like very much to see you."

"I would rather not see him," said Catherine quickly.

"I met him at Marian's, and they are so afraid you will meet him there. I think that's why he goes. He wants so much to see you." Catherine said nothing and Mrs Penniman went on. "He is still very handsome, but of course he looks older. Things have not gone well for him, he has been all over the world, but his evil star was against him. I believe he married a lady in Europe, but she died shortly after. The first thing he did was to ask me about you. He heard that you had never married and he seemed very interested in this. He said you had been the real romance of his life."

Catherine stared at the ground and listened silently. "Please say no more."

"But he wants so much to see you."

"Please don't, Aunt Lavinia," said Catherine getting up from her seat. She moved quickly to the other window, which was open to the balcony. Her aunt could not see her behind the white curtains. She was trembling and her heart was beating loudly. Feelings that she thought were dead began to stir. [1] Then suddenly she burst into tears, silent tears that Mrs Penniman could not see, but suspected.

A week passed and one evening as they sat in the front parlour Mrs Penniman suddenly said, "Morris has sent you a message. He wishes to see you. He says his happiness depends on it."

"My happiness does not," said Catherine.

"He is going away again. He has something very important to say to you. He believes that you never understood him and that you never judged him in the right way. He wishes to meet you as a friend."

Catherine listened to this wonderful speech without looking up from her embroidery. [2] Then she said simply, "Please say to Mr Townsend that I wish he would leave me alone."

She had just finished speaking when the door bell rang. Catherine looked up at the clock; it was a quarter past nine—a very late hour for visitors. Catherine's eyes turned quickly to her aunt, who was blushing.

"Aunt Penniman," she said, in a tone that frightened her companion, "what have you done?"

---

1. **stir** : move about.
2. **embroidery** : ornamental needlework (sewing).

The Will

"My dearest Catherine," stammered [1] Mrs Penniman, "just wait until you see him!"

Catherine had frightened her aunt but she was also frightened, and before she could do something, the servant had opened the door and announced his name.

"Mr Morris Townsend."

She heard the name and she stood with her back to the door of the parlour. She remained still, [2] feeling that he had come in. He had not spoken, however, and at last she turned around. There, she saw a gentleman standing in the middle of the room, from which her aunt had discreetly left.

She would never have recognized him. He was forty-five years old. He was fatter, his hair was thin and he had a thick beard.

"I have come—I have come," he said and then he paused, looking around him, as if he expected her to ask him to sit down. It was the old voice but it did not have the old charm.

Morris was embarrassed but Catherine gave him no help. How could she welcome him when she did not want him to come?

"I wanted to so much—I was determined," Morris went on. Catherine continued to look at him and made the strangest observation: this was the man who had been everything, and yet

---

1. **stammered** : spoke with repeated sounds and pauses, often caused by nervousness or excitement.
2. **still** : *(here)* without moving.

this person was nothing. How long ago it was, how old she had grown, how much she had lived! The story of his life was written in his eyes—he had made himself comfortable and he had never been caught. His presence was painful to her and she wished he would go.

"I think it was wrong of you to come," said Catherine.

"Did Mrs Penniman give you my message?"

"She told me something but I did not understand."

"I wish you would let *me* tell you."

"I don't think it is necessary," said Catherine.

"Not for you, perhaps, but for me." He seemed to be coming nearer and Catherine turned away. "Can't we be friends again?"

"We are not enemies," said Catherine.

He moved closer to her. She saw his beard and the eyes above it, looking strange and hard. It was very different from his old— from his young—face. "Catherine," he murmured, "I have never stopped thinking of you."

"Please don't say these things," she answered.

"If my presence troubles you, I will go away; but you must let me come again."

"Please don't come again," she said. "It is wrong of you. There is no reason for it. You have treated me badly."

"That is not true. You had your quiet life with your father, which I did not want to rob from you."

"Yes, I had that."

Morris knew about Doctor Sloper's will and about the property she had inherited, but he said nothing.

"Catherine, have you forgiven me?"

"I forgave you years ago, but it is useless for us to try to be friends."

"We can forget the past. We still have a future."

"I can't forget—I don't forget," said Catherine. "You treated me too badly. I felt it very much for years. I can't begin again. Everything is dead and buried. It was too serious; it made a great change in my life. I never expected to see you here."

Morris looked at her and asked, "Why have you never married?"

"I didn't wish to marry."

"Yes, you are rich, you are free. Marriage had nothing to offer you." Morris looked vaguely around him, gave a deep sigh and said, "Well, I had hoped that we could still be friends."

"There is no possibility of that," said Catherine.

"Good-bye, then," said Morris.

She stood there, looking at the ground after she had heard him close the door of the room.

In the hall he found Mrs Penniman, curious and eager.

"That was a precious plan of yours!" said Morris.

"Is she so hard?" asked Mrs Penniman.

"She doesn't care a button for me," said Morris. "But why, then, has she never married?"

"Yes, why?" sighed Mrs Penniman. "But you will not give up—you will come back?"

"Come back! Certainly not!" And Morris Townsend walked out of the house, leaving Mrs Penniman staring.

Washington Square

Catherine, meanwhile, in the parlour, picking up her
embroidery, had seated herself with it again—for life, as it were.

Comprehension and personal response

1 **a.** How has Doctor Sloper changed his will?

b. What does Catherine think of the changes? Is she disappointed?

c. Where did Mrs Penniman meet Morris?

d. What has happened to him in the meantime?

e. Does Catherine still feel something for Morris? Does she want to meet him?

f. What does Catherine discover when she meets Morris again? Choose an answer among those given below:

  i. He is no longer important to her.

  ii. She dislikes his physical changes.

  iii. She hasn't forgiven him and wants her revenge.

g. How does the story end for the two main characters?

Morris:

  i. regrets he had not appreciated Catherine's love in the past.

  ii. is furious he has been rejected and will not try again.

  iii. will try to win Catherine back.

Catherine:

  i. chooses and accepts solitude.

  ii. has discovered she still has feelings for him.

  iii. can now forget Morris and fall in love with somebody else.

Food for thought

2 The end of the story is very sad and everybody has lost something. Find at least one thing that each of the main characters has lost.

Language production

3 Could the story have taken a different turn if you had been the author? Try to write a different ending for the last chapter of *Washington Square*.

Listening

 4 Try and put the following sentences in their correct order and then listen to the first two paragraphs on the CD. As you listen, put the sentences below in the correct sequence.

   a. When his will was opened it was discovered that he had changed it shortly before his death.

   b. He left the rest of his fortune to several different hospitals and schools of medicine in various cities.

   c. Another year passed and Doctor Sloper became very ill.

   d. Mrs Penniman thought that the will was cruel and unjust, but Catherine simply said, "I like it very much. I only wish it had been expressed differently."

   e. Catherine received only a fifth of his property.

   f. After a three-week illness, during which Catherine and Mrs Penniman were always at his bedside, he died.

   g. "She is well provided from her mother's side," the will read, "her fortune is already more than sufficient to attract those unscrupulous adventurers whom she regards as an interesting class."

EXIT TEST

Focus on the context

1 **Answer the following questions.**

   a. Who was the author of *Washington Square*?

   b. When and where was he born?

   c. After leaving the United States, where did he go?

   d. Who was his supreme literary master?

   e. Name three of his works.

   f. Who sold Manhattan Island to Peter Minuit in 1626?

   g. What did New York offer European immigrants during the 19th century?

SCORE ⬤⬤⬤ **/7**

Focus on the story

FCE **2** **For questions 1 – 15, choose the correct answers (A, B, C or D).**

   1. **Doctor Sloper was**

      A an unscrupulous doctor.

      B the richest doctor in New York City.

      C an intelligent, honest doctor.

      D disliked by his patients.

   2. **His daughter, Catherine Sloper, was**

      A rich and beautiful.

      B very ill and weak.

      C stubborn and impolite.

      D dull, plain and shy.

   3. **Mrs Lavinia Penniman was**

      A Morris Townsend's aunt.

      B Catherine's grandmother.

      C Dr Sloper's servant.

      D Dr Sloper's sister.

4. **Morris Townsend was a**

   A   handsome, clever young man.

   B   young doctor.

   C   rich, handsome actor.

   D   good friend of Doctor Sloper's.

5. **Dr Sloper invited Morris Townsend to dinner and decided that**

   A   he was a mysterious man.

   B   he was completely insincere.

   C   he was very lazy.

   D   he was in love with Catherine.

6. **Catherine Sloper never told her father**

   A   that she gave Morris a lot of money.

   B   that she went out with Morris.

   C   about Morris's numerous visits.

   D   about her new, expensive evening dress.

7. **Dr Sloper didn't want Catherine to marry Morris because**

   A   he was not a doctor.

   B   he was a foreigner.

   C   he was too old for her.

   D   he was only interested in her money.

8. **Morris Townsend's sister, Mrs Montgomery,**

   A   agreed with Dr Sloper's opinion of Morris.

   B   said many good things about Morris.

   C   hadn't seen Morris for eight years.

   D   was a very rich woman.

9. **What advice did Mrs Penniman give Morris at the oyster saloon?**

   A   "Write Dr Sloper a long letter."

   B   "Marry Catherine and go to Europe."

   C   "Marry Catherine first and tell him after!"

   D   "Leave Catherine alone!"

10. If Catherine married Morris without her father's consent,

    A Mrs Penniman would be responsible.

    B she would have to leave New York.

    C he would never speak to her again.

    D she would not receive any of his money after his death.

11. When Catherine returned from Europe

    A she did not want to get married.

    B her father agreed to the marriage with Morris.

    C her character had changed.

    D Mrs Penniman was very ill.

12. Morris Townsend broke off his engagement to Catherine

    A because he loved another girl.

    B because he did not want to marry a girl who was not rich or attractive.

    C and went to California.

    D because he respected Doctor Sloper's wishes.

13. How did Catherine react to Morris's decision?

    A She suffered tremendously.

    B She was indifferent.

    C She was happy.

    D She quarrelled with her father day and night.

14. When Dr Sloper died, Catherine received

    A all of his property.

    B a fifth of his property.

    C a quarter of his property.

    D none of his property.

15. When Catherine met Morris after many years

    A she rejected him but she still loved him.

    B she insulted him.

    C she rejected him and chose her solitude.

    D she refused to speak to him.

3 **Match the word with its meaning.**

1.	quarrel	**a.**	not healthy
2.	awkward	**b.**	crime of disloyalty or betrayal
3.	sickly	**c.**	courageous
4.	dreadful	**d.**	very difficult situation
5.	treason	**e.**	stupid, not sensible
6.	foolish	**f.**	argument, dispute
7.	brave	**g.**	occupation
8.	envious	**h.**	difficult, embarrassing
9.	employment	**i.**	terrible, horrible
10.	mess	**j.**	jealous

Washington Square

KEY TO
THE ACTIVITIES
AND EXIT TEST

A Note on Henry James

Exercise 1, page 12

e / a / f / b / d / g / h / c

Chapter 1 – Doctor Sloper

Exercise 1, page 19

a. F – He lived in New York.   **b.** T
c. T   **d.** F – Nobody criticised him but himself.   **e.** F – Mrs Almond was his favourite sister.   **f.** F – He wanted her to be clever.   **g.** T
h. F – She completely lacked her mother's beauty.   **i.** T   **j.** T

Exercise 2, page 19

a. Suggested answer: Doctor Sloper could be described as being intelligent, elegant, distinguished etc. but he also seems to be very proud, self-centred and critical, particularly towards his daughter.
b. Doctor Sloper's disappointment is clearly stated in the paragraphs beginning: "Although Catherine never knew it…" and "As the years passed…" (p.18).

c. Suggested answer: Catherine's character could be described as being good-natured and docile, although she was very shy and insecure. Her relationship with her father was probably quite one-sided as she was always looking to please him. She probably couldn't understand his "coldness" towards her.
d. Catherine: robust, healthy, not romantic, well built, large, not clever, not ugly, good, docile, obedient, affectionate, not pretty, not elegant, not charming, quiet, insignificant, lady-like, polite, dull, plain, irresponsive, shy. Doctor Sloper: intelligent, honest, skilled, clever, astute, proud. Mrs Penniman: tall, thin, fair, romantic, sentimental.

Exercise 3, page 20

honest / dishonest
honourable / dishonourable
beautiful / ugly
successful / unsuccessful
romantic / practical, unromantic

169

thin / fat, large
healthy / unhealthy, sickly
reasonable / unreasonable
clever / dumb, stupid
plain / smart, pretty
bright / dull
charming / boring, uninteresting
shy / self confident
robust / frail
tall / short
fair / dark
large / small, thin
obedient / disobedient
ugly / beautiful, pretty
dull / bright

Exercise 4, page 20

Possible examples:

Infinitive	Past Simple	Past Participle
to live	lived	lived
to have	had	had
to make	made	made
to fall	fell	fallen
to bear	bore	borne
to grow	grew	grown
to die	died	died
to go	went	gone
to feel	felt	felt
to ask	asked	asked
to say	said	said

Chapter 2
An Important Encounter

Exercise 1, page 26

a. Suggested answer: She wanted to compensate for her plainness.
b. **Physical aspect:** handsome, tall, slim, strong
   Character: clever, amusing, sincere, natural
c. Suggested answer: It seems that Catherine is very attracted to him, as can be seen from the

quotes below.
"Catherine sat in her place with her eyes fixed upon him, smiling, thinking he was very clever and admiring his delicate features." (pp. 23-24)
"It seemed to Catherine that no one who had seen him would ever forget him." (p. 24)
"Catherine was completely absorbed by Morris Townsend. He was very amusing and she had never heard anyone speak as well as he did." (p. 24)
d./e. Open answers.

Exercise 2, pages 26-27

a. finally   b. overdressed
c. evening dress   d. saving
e. to move   f. life still had a rural flavour   g. appropriate
h. became engaged

Exercise 3, page 27

a. had never tried
b. had already had
c. had just come back
d. had already left
e. had already gone out

Chapter 3 – New Feelings

Exercise 1, page 32

a. She danced with one of the Almond boys. She probably didn't get dizzy because she wasn't attracted to him.
b. She is very complementary about him using adjectives such as: handsome, clever, charming.
c. Not especially. He thinks that Morris liked the dress because it

looked expensive.

d. She reveals them by the way she answers her father in the carriage "Well, he is!" (p. 31)

Exercise 2, page 32

a. conceited **b.** amazed
c. magnificent **d.** opulent
e. carriage **f.** refined **g.** romance

Exercise 3, page 33

c / a / e / g / d / f / b

Exercise 4, page 33

a. Marian Almond asked Catherine what she thought of Morris.
b. Catherine implored her cousin not to tell him.
c. He asked if that magnificent person was his child.
d. Doctor Sloper asked his sister who the young man she had talked with for so long was.
e. Her aunt declared (that) he was very handsome, clever and charming.
f. Mrs Penniman said (that) she didn't believe he thought of that.
g. Doctor Sloper thought (that) the hour had come.

Chapter 4
A Late Autumn Afternoon

Exercise 1, page 38

a. Suggested answer: Arthur Townsend is Morris's cousin and the future husband of Catherine's cousin, Marian Almond. Although little is said about him, he seems to be very self-confident, somewhat superficial and quite smug.

b. See the conversation between Catherine and Arthur Townsend from "Ah, if he can find something to do" to "He hasn't got a father – he has only got a sister" (p. 36).

c. Suggested answer: In those times it was not considered acceptable for men to approach women immediately; they would spend time in the society of an elder relative before. There may have been another motive: Morris may have asked his cousin to find out what Catherine thought of him.

d. "...I can't say that we didn't talk about Miss Sloper." (p. 36)

e. i.

Exercise 2, page 38

a. to pay a short visit; to go to somebody's house, office etc; to stop at.

b. call round; call on; drop in.

Exercise 3, page 39

Present Progressive: he is looking around; we are talking; I'm not talking; he is coming.
Future: he was getting married soon
Past Progressive: Catherine and her aunt were sitting; She kept looking over and … was listening; Mr Townsend and her aunt were saying; they were making fun of her; Morris Townsend stood looking at her and smiling; Catherine was still blushing.

Exercise 4, page 39

Open answer.

Chapter 5 – A Surprise Visit

Exercise 1, page 43

a. No, he didn't. He seemed a bit annoyed.

b. He came five days later.

c. Likes: Catherine: the theatre, operatic music / Morris: natural things; music
Dislikes: Catherine: literature / Morris: books, actors, authors

d. Suggested answer: Catherine could only think that "some other time" had a delightful sound; it seemed to indicate other meetings in the future.

e. No, she didn't want to tell her father but she felt obliged to do so. She was most likely aware that he wouldn't favour the visit and that he would make fun of her.

Exercise 2, page 43

a. drawing room, living room, sitting room
modern words: living room, sitting room, lounge.
a shop or type of business that provides a particular service: ice cream parlour; beauty parlour; funeral parlour; etc.

b. to propose to = to ask someone to marry you (formal) / "Well, my dear, did he ask you to marry him today?"

Exercise 3, page 44

a. F – His first name was Austin.
b. F – He seemed more at ease this time. **c.** T **d.** T **e.** T
f. F – He says, "My daughter is definitely not brilliant." (p. 42)

Chapter 6
An Important Dinner

Exercise 1, page 52

a. F – Doctor Sloper decided to ask Elizabeth. **b.** F – She is not very rich and she has five children.
c. T **d.** T **e.** T **f.** F – Doctor Sloper did not expect his daughter to marry a rich man. **g.** F – Doctor Sloper wanted Morris to be invited to dinner. **h.** T **i.** F – Catherine preferred not to know whether her father liked Morris. **j.** F – Doctor Sloper was able to make a judgement almost immediately.

Exercise 2, pages 52-53

a. Suggested answer: Mrs Almond could be described as being kind, well-balanced, understanding, compassionate and practical.

b. Mrs Montgomery, widow; five; a little property; Second Avenue

c. Suggested answer: He wants to meet Morris so he can understand what the young man's intentions are.

d. good points: self-confident, clever, charming with the ladies, handsome
bad points: not a gentleman, insincere

Exercise 3, page 53

a. find out **b.** look for **c.** come back **d.** come along **e.** get up
f. look at **g.** see through

Exercise 4, page 54

a. "Catherine has her own style" to "...the age of calculation" (p. 47)

b. "Your father doesn't like me … I feel these things" (p. 50)

c. "Ah, well, I must try to make him like me" (p. 51)

Exercise 5, page 54

a. Morris

b. Doctor Sloper

c. Mrs Almond

Chapter 7
Catherine is in Love

Exercise 1, page 59

a. Catherine is happy because she is falling in love with Morris.

b. Catherine hides her feelings, especially from her father.

c. The silence regarding Morris irritates Doctor Sloper.

d. Yes, Aunt Penniman believes that Catherine is very much in love.

e. She thinks that Morris is interested in Catherine's "lovely nature".

f. Being alone in the world, being betrayed by false friends.

g. She tells her brother that Catherine is not weak / Open Answer.

Exercise 2, page 59

a. Suggested answer: Doctor Sloper is an intelligent, brilliant man professionally. However, with regards to his personal behaviour he can be described as being bitter, mean, suspicious and cold.

b. bitter/sweet; intelligent/stupid; mean/generous; superficial/deep;

suspicious/trusting; disappointed/enthusiastic; affectionate/cold; brilliant/dull.

Exercise 3, page 59

Open answer.

Exercise 4, page 60

a. therefore **b.** as **c.** as a result
d. because **e.** unless **f.** so

Chapter 8 – Morris Townsend and the Doctor

Exercise 1, page 66

a. From: "The Doctor almost pitied her" to: "I should give him another chance." (p. 62)

b. i. (ii. can also be considered correct)

c. Suggested answer: The statement can also be interpreted as referring to whether Morris will be able to gain the Doctor's approval in the future.

d. Mrs Montgomery / He wants to learn more about Townsend's character.

Exercise 2, page 66

a. ugly: unpleasant to look at; unattractive

b. brave: having no fear; fearless

c. stupid: with a low level of intelligence; dumb

d. inanimate: lacking any sign of life; spiritless; lifeless

e. poor: having little money; penniless

f. handsome: pleasant to look at; attractive; good-looking

g. proud: feeling of being satisfied with yourself; having a high opinion of yourself; haughty

Exercise 3, page 67

a. am told **b.** would like to find
c. not to give up **d.** how would you feel **e.** I doubt it **f.** it isn't a career

Exercise 4, page 67

a. must
b. would/could/might
c. could/would
d. should

Chapter 9 – The Proposal

Exercise 1a, page 75

a. F – Mrs Penniman left the young people alone. **b.** F – Morris had kissed Catherine on his last visit.
c. T **d.** T **e.** F – Morris asked Catherine if she would remain faithful to him. **f.** F – He was sitting in his chair, beside the fire.
g. F – He was startled when he heard the news. **h.** T **i.** T **j.** T

Exercise 1b, page 76

a. Catherine and Morris decide to get married.
b. Morris says that Catherine's father will think that he is only interested in her fortune and in fact the money will be a burden on them.
c. She is happy that they will be rich.
d. She has known it for five days.
e. He accuses him of leading a life of dissipation and spending his own fortune.
f. Suggested answer: He will probably refuse to give his consent to the marriage.

Exercise 2, page 76

a. "She worried that her father would not like Morris Townsend." (p. 69)
b. "Morris," she said suddenly, "are you very sure you love me?" (p. 70)
c. "She saw … his smile. She looked back at the fire; it was much warmer." (p. 72)
d. "I am afraid that you will soon feel older and wiser. I don't like your engagement." (p. 73)
e. "There was something hopeless and oppressive in arguing with her father." (p. 74)

Exercise 3, page 77

a. Old fashioned words:
Betrothed (adj.), *betrothal* (n) = engaged to be married; *Courtship* = period when a couple are getting to know each other before deciding to get married.
Fiancé = a man who is engaged to be married; *Fiancée* = a woman who is engaged to be married. Both are still in use but are considered quite formal.
b. Possible additional words: ceremony; vows; reception; honeymoon; anniversary; best-man; bridesmaids.
The following are considered very informal: tie the knot; get hitched; walk down the aisle; take the plunge.

Exercise 4, page 77

Open answer.

New York City in the 1850's

Exercise 1, page 84

a. F – New York developed rapidly.
b. F – The Dutch West India Company bought Manhattan Island from the Indians.   **c.** T   **d.** F – The northern part of New York became an elegant residential area.
e. T   **f.** T   **g.** F – In the 19th century three quarters of immigrants chose to live in New York City.
h. T

Chapter 10
Doctor Sloper's Decision

Exercise 1, page 90

a. No, he isn't. He is quite relaxed.
b. iii.
c. Morris is not in the same social class as Catherine and, more importantly, he believes that Morris is only interested in her fortune.
d. Mrs Penniman (Chapter 7 p. 58) / Open answer.
e. Morris is offering "tender affection and life-long devotion" (p. 88) / Open answer.
f. Doctor Sloper thinks it will take Catherine one year to forget Morris / Morris answers that she will never forget him.

Exercise 2, page 90

a. Adjectives: poor; penniless.
Nouns: position; resources; prospects; large fortune; money; economy, extravagance.
Verb: to spend.
b. Open answer.
Possible additional examples:
Nouns: Cash; funds; banknotes; coins; change; legal tender; riches; bank account.
Adjectives: wealthy; affluent; bankrupt; destitute.
Verbs: to save; to buy.
Informal / slang: dough; dosh; loaded; stingy; broke.

Exercise 3, page 91

a. he would marry   **b.** they wouldn't live   **c.** he would still have
d. she would be   **e.** wouldn't help
f. he wouldn't make

Exercise 4, page 91

b / d / a / e / c / f

Chapter 11
Mrs Montgomery

Exercise 1, page 95

a. T   **b.** T   **c.** T   **d.** F – She would still have the ten thousand pounds from her mother.   **e.** T
f. F – She thinks that he is selfish but that he hides it very well.
g. F – Mrs Montgomery gives her brother money.   **h.** T

Exercise 2, page 95

a. ii.
b. Open answer.

Exercise 3, page 96

a. Mrs Montgomery can be described as being not very tall with blonde hair and blue eyes.
b. Open answer.

c. Avenue: wide street with buildings on one or both sides; road with trees on each side.
Street: a public road in a city or town.
Road: a specially prepared hard surface for cars, buses etc.
Highway: a main road that joins one town to another.
Toll Road: a road that you pay to use.
Lane: a narrow road in the countryside.
Alley: a narrow street between buildings.
Square: a space in a town with buildings around it, usually in the shape of a square.
Circus: a round open space in a town where several streets meet.
Crescent: a street with a curved shape.

Exercise 4, page 97

received / was / was / talk / can understand / may be / said / understand / wishes / marry / wish / find out / is / have come / ask / depends / is a / understand / murmured / must remind / will have / marries / approve / will be / said / marries / will have / inherited / will / have

Chapter 12 – Mrs Penniman's Secret Meeting

Exercise 1, page 105

e / a / f / b / h / d / g / c

Exercise 2, page 105

a. Suggested answer: He would have liked her to show her

emotions, show that she had some character. The situation also amused him.

b. Suggested answer: Mrs Penniman was promoting the match; encouraging both Morris and Catherine.

c. Catherine's attitude towards her father is of obedience.

d. i. Morris Townsend
ii. Mrs Penniman
iii. Doctor Sloper

Exercise 3, page 106

Open answer.

Exercise 4, page 106

a. "The letter … was also long for Morris." (p. 99)

b. "she is true to you until death." (p. 101)

c. "He thought it was a wonderfully comfortable house." (p. 102)

d. "Why do you push me so?" (p. 104)

Chapter 13
The Confrontation

Exercise 1, page 113

a. Catherine sat alone by the parlour fire for more than an hour.

b. She waited silently before speaking. He returned to his desk and started writing.

c. i, ii and iii.

d. Yes.

e. No, he didn't. He had already made his judgment. We can see this from the quotes below.
"He has never done anything – he is selfish and lazy." (p. 105)
"I know him well enough, and I

will never consent." (p. 110)
"I shall never speak to him again.
I dislike him too much." (p. 110)
f. No, she wanted to see Morris.
g. She was crying when she left the room.
h. No, He was a little irritated but he also found it a bit amusing.

Exercise 2, page 113

Suggested answer: A father in Doctor Sloper's position would probably feel anxious, sympathetic, pained and sad. However, in the text it states that Doctor Sloper felt irritated and amused, which is the complete opposite to what we might expect. It clearly illustrates how little his regard for Catherine is.

Exercise 3, page 114

by the parlour fire / aggressive and foolish / a horrible thing / go on with it / the door of the library / a ghost / went back to his writing desk / of his pen

Exercise 4, page 114

a. If Catherine had been beautiful, maybe Morris would have loved her.
b. Her father would have been pleased, if Catherine had left Morris.
c. If Morris hadn't been lazy, he wouldn't have needed a rich wife.
d. If Doctor Sloper had understood how unhappy his daughter was, he wouldn't have opposed her marriage.
e. Mrs Penniman would have advised Catherine better if she hadn't been foolish.

f. If Doctor Sloper had liked Morris, he would have given his consent to the marriage.

Chapter 14
Catherine Chooses
Exercise 1, page 121

b / g / i / a / f / e / h / d / c

Exercise 2, pages 121-122

a. deliver   **b.** blush   **c.** treason
d. distinguished   **e.** eyebrows
f. forgive   **g.** amusement
h. offence

Exercise 3, pages 122-123

1. coldness   **2.** secret   **3.** door
4. messenger   **5.** annoyed
6. advised   **7.** less   **8.** agreed
9. upset   **10.** raised

Exercise 4, page 123

Open answer.

Chapter 15 – Europe
Exercise 1, page 131

a. Suggested answer: No, he wasn't. This is why he proposed taking Catherine away to Europe.
b. Yes. It told her that her father was still interested in her welfare.
c. Suggested answer: Mrs Penniman wasn't invited because she would continue to give Catherine encouragement.
d. Suggested answer: Catherine was only going to Europe to please her father; at another time she probably would have liked what she saw better, however, she had Morris and her future marriage always on her mind.

e. Morris advised her to go in the hope that her father may change his mind.

f. They stayed in Europe for twelve months.

g. They discussed the situation twice: firstly after six months while walking in the alps and secondly, before leaving to sail back to New York.

h. Doctor Sloper asked Catherine what she was going to do when she got home.

i. Mrs Penniman had continued to see Morris. Mrs Almond had not approved. She had told her sister to stop behaving foolishly.

j. Suggested answer: No, she was no longer concerned. She had given up trying to please her father as she had realised that it was hopeless.

Exercise 2, page 131

quiet, dull, docile, punctual, obedient, unintelligent, brave, handsome, sharper, authoritative. The latter adjectives show that she has changed considerably. This does, however, correspond with Morris and Mrs Penniman's claims of her not being weak.

Exercise 3, pages 131-132

"go off" / her aunt / passion and energy / used to sit / were in Europe / be so friendly / to her / found some employment / a partnership

Exercise 4, page 132

a. Catherine wished (that) Morris had found employment.

b. Catherine wished (that) her father had been more gentle to her.

c. Mrs Penniman wished (that) her brother had changed his mind.

d. Morris wished (that) Catherine had been interested in Europe.

e. Mrs Penniman wished (that) Morris hadn't cared about money.

f. Doctor Sloper wished (that) Catherine hadn't written to Morris.

Chapter 16
Morris's Decision

Exercise 1, page 137

a. F – He didn't notice any improvement. **b.** F – She brought the subject up. **c.** T **d.** F – He had been very fond of Catherine's mother. **e.** T **f.** T **g.** F – Mrs Almond said that Catherine would never give Morris up. **h.** T
i. F – He felt vicious and cruel.
j. F – Mrs Penniman told Morris that he should visit and tell her in person.

Exercise 2, page 138

a. Suggested answer: Catherine is more self-confident, which is probably a result of the change in her relationship with her father.

b. ii.

Exercise 3, page 138

Open answer.
Possible additional examples:
Positive: pretty; stunning; striking; nice-looking; elegant; smart; appealing
Negative: unattractive; plain

Exercise 4, page 139

a. who   **b.** whose   **c.** no relative necessary   **d.** whom   **e.** which
f. whose   **g.** whom, who

Exercise 5, page 139

a. "...it didn't appear afterward that he found her more attractive." (p. 133)
b. "...He was so fond of my mother ... He is always thinking of her. (p. 134)
c. "Morris was ashamed of himself. He felt vicious and cruel." (p. 136)
d. "...I have been to see her four times since she came back, and it is very hard work." (p. 136)

Chapter 17 – The Parting

Exercise 1, page 146

e / c / g / d / h / a / f / b

Exercise 2, pages 146-147

a. i
b. iii

Exercise 3, page 147

Open answer.

Exercise 4, page 147

a. get away   **b.** give up   **c.** go away   **d.** wait for   **e.** break off
f. put off

Exercise 5, page 148

a. waiting for   **b.** given up
c. putting ... off   **d.** broken off
e. go away   **f.** get away

Exercise 6, page 148

c / b / e / a / d

Chapter 18 – The Letter

Exercise 1, page 153

a. F – Morris sent Catherine a long letter from Philadelphia.   **b.** T
c. T   **d.** F – Catherine hid the truth from her father.   **e.** F – She received two offers.   **f.** F – She accepted life as a single woman.
g. T   **h.** F – He asked her to promise that she wouldn't marry him.   **i.** T   **j.** T

Exercise 2, pages 153-154

a. Mrs Almond.
b. Suggested answer:
Good points: protective, firm
Negative points: unsympathetic, judgmental.
c. Her father's low opinion of her.

Exercise 3, page 154

a. Open answer.
b. Suggested answer: Catherine has become much more confident / Proud, Obstinate / less naive and colder.

Exercise 4, pages 154-155

1. offers   **2.** widower   **3.** clever
4. suspected   **5.** maid   **6.** played
7. dead   **8.** respectable

Exercise 5, page 155

a. As   **b.** However   **c.** but
d. after   **e.** although/while

Chapter 19 – The Will

Exercise 1, page 163

a. Charlotte was to inherit only a fifth of his fortune.
b. She is satisfied with the changes; she didn't expect more from her father.

c. At Marian's.

d. He has travelled all over the world; he has been widowed.

e. She still has feelings for Morris but she dreaded meeting him.

f. i.

g. Morris: ii
Catherine: i

Exercise 2, page 164

Suggested answer:
Catherine: She lost Morris and her affection for her father.

Morris: Catherine's love and her fortune.
Doctor Sloper: His daughter's love.

Exercise 3, page 164

Open answer.

Exercise 4, page 164

c / f / a / e / g / b / d

KEY TO THE EXIT TEST

Focus on the context

a. Henry James.

b. He was born on 15 April 1843 in New York.

c. He went to Europe.

d. Balzac.

e. *Daisy Miller, Portrait of a Lady, The Bostonians, The Wings of the Dove, The Golden Bowl, The Awkward Age, The Ambassadors.*

f. The American Indians.

g. All kinds of work in industry and business.

Focus on the story

2

1. C 2. D 3. D 4. A 5. B 6. C
7. D 8. A 9. C 10. D 11. C
12. B 13. A 14. B 15. C

3

1. f 2. h 3. a 4. i 5. b 6. e
7. c 8. j 9. g 10. d

Notes

Notes

Black Cat English Readers

Level 1
Peter Pan
Zorro!
American Folk Tales
The True Story of Pocahontas
Davy Crockett

Level 2
Oliver Twist
King Arthur and his Knights
Oscar Wilde's Short Stories
Robin Hood
British and American
  Festivities

Level 3
Alice's Adventures in
  Wonderland
The Jumping Frog
Hamlet
The Secret Garden
Great English Monarchs and
  their Times

Level 4
The £1,000,000 Bank Note
Jane Eyre
Sherlock Holmes Investigates
Gulliver's Travels
The Strange Case of Dr Jekyll
  and Mr Hyde
Classic Detective Stories
The Phantom of the Opera
Alien at School
Romeo and Juliet
Treasure Island

Level 5
A Christmas Carol
The Tragedy of Dr Faustus
Washington Square
A Midsummer Night's Dream
American Horror
Much Ado About Nothing
The Canterbury Tales
Dracula
The Last of the Mohicans
The Big Mistake and Other
  Stories

Level 6
Frankenstein
Pride and Prejudice
Robinson Crusoe
A Tale of Two Cities
The X-Files : Squeeze

BLACK CAT ENGLISH CLUB

Membership Application Form

BLACK CAT ENGLISH CLUB is for those who love English reading and seek for better English to share and learn with fun together.

Benefits offered: - *Membership Card*

- *Member badge, poster, bookmark*

- *Book discount coupon*

- *Black Cat English Reward Scheme*

- *English learning e-forum*

- *Surprise gift and more...*

Simply fill out the application form below and fax it back to **2565 1113**.

Join Now! It's FREE exclusively for readers who have purchased *Black Cat English Readers* !

The book(or book set) that you have purchased: _____

English Name:_____ (Surname) _____ (Given Name)

Chinese Name: _____

Address: _____

Tel: _____ Fax: _____

Email:_____
(Login password for e-forum will be sent to this email address.)

Sex: ❏ Male   ❏ Female

Education Background: ❏ Primary 1-3   ❏ Primary 4-6   ❏ Junior Secondary Education (F1-3)

❏ Senior Secondary Education (F4-5)   ❏ Matriculation

❏ College   ❏ University or above

Age: ❏ 6 - 9   ❏ 10 - 12   ❏ 13 - 15   ❏ 16 - 18   ❏ 19 - 24   ❏ 25 - 34

❏ 35 - 44   ❏ 45 - 54   ❏ 55 or above

Occupation: ❏ Student   ❏ Teacher   ❏ White Collar   ❏ Blue Collar

❏ Professional   ❏ Manager   ❏ Business Owner   ❏ Housewife

❏ Others (please specify: _____)

As a member, what would you like **BLACK CAT ENGLISH CLUB** to offer:

❏ Member gathering/ party   ❏ English class with native teacher   ❏ English competition

❏ Newsletter   ❏ Online sharing   ❏ Book fair

❏ Book discount   ❏ Others (please specify: _____)

Other suggestions to **BLACK CAT ENGLISH CLUB**:

_____

Please sign here: _____

(Date: _____)